HANI
ALONGSIDI
and Oth. ...ıes

HAND IN HAND
ALONGSIDE THE TRACKS
and Other Stories

CONTEMPORARY ARGENTINE STORIES

Edited by
Norman Thomas di Giovanni

Translated by
Norman Thomas di Giovanni and Susan Ashe

CONSTABLE · LONDON

First published in Great Britain 1992
by Constable and Company Limited
3 The Lanchesters, 162 Fulham Palace Road
London W6 9ER
Selection, introduction, and notes copyright © 1992
by Norman Thomas di Giovanni
English translations copyright © 1987, 1991, 1992
by Norman Thomas di Giovanni and Susan Ashe
The right of Norman Thomas di Giovanni to be
identified as the author of this work has been
asserted by him in accordance with the Copyright,
Designs and Patents Act 1988
ISBN 0 09 470800 2 hbk
ISBN 0 09 471540 8 pbk
Set in 11pt Imprint
and printed in Great Britain by
Redwood Press Limited
Melksham, Wiltshire

A CIP catalogue record for this book
is available from the British Library

TO EDWARD AND MARIA SHAW
in memory of Argentine hospitality

Contents

Acknowledgements

Certain of these stories have appeared previously in *Translation* and *The American Voice* in the United States, and in *Index on Censorship* in Great Britain.

'Palisava' has been broadcast on the BBC World Service.

Once again thanks are due to the Fundación Antorchas, Buenos Aires, for their assistance.

I am also grateful to Andrew Graham-Yooll for kindly badgering as well as for every sort of help. And to Natu Poblet, Celia Szusterman, Juan Antonio Masoliver, Jason Wilson, Juan Forn, my sons Thomas and Derek di Giovanni, Derek Birdsall, and Miriam Frank. And to the following old and new London and Buenos Aires friends and benefactors: Guillermo and Hersilia Peña, Margaret Murray, Washington Pereyra, Daniel Martínez, Teddy Paz, Christopher and Diana Stobart, Francesca von Thielmann, and Jean-Louis Larivière.

The Argentine painter Luis Fernando Benedit kindly gave permission for his water-colour *Para don Florencio (calentando el horno) 3* to be reproduced on the jacket; Laura Batkis and the Ruth Benzacar Galería de Arte in Buenos Aires were generous too in their assistance.

N T di G

Introduction

My initiation into Argentine literature began at the deep end. Twenty-odd years ago, almost literally before I had read any of it, I was translating that part of it which was written by Jorge Luis Borges – at Borges's side in Buenos Aires. Thanks to him, before I had read any of them, I was meeting all the establishment figures of literary Argentina – Adolfo Bioy-Casares, Silvina Ocampo, José Bianco, Victoria Ocampo, Eduardo Mallea, Manuel Mujica Laínez, Enrique Pezzoni, Manuel Peyroux, Ernesto Sábato, and so forth. Borges, to whom literature was always a joy, an adventure, was the best possible guide. He was for ever giving me books, pushing me towards this or that writer's work, and encouraging me not to be daunted by the classics of Argentine literature, especially those of the last century.

I confess that it was years before I could see the forest for the ombus, the jacarandas, and the eucalyptuses. My introduction to gauchesco writers, to *Martín Fierro*, to Sarmiento, to the issues between *unitarios* and *federales* – to the story of the Argentine Republic itself – was as a bewildered onlooker in the front row of dim or draughty or sweltering public halls in Casilda, Coronel Pringles, Tres Arroyos, or any of the other numerous small pampa towns where I accompanied the Master on his indefatigable lectures. There are passages of José Hernández that I must have heard him recite fifty times – always out of any possible context for me – yet to this day I have only to recall the outlaws Cruz and Fierro looking back on the last settlements as they flee into the wilderness, the latter with two big tears rolling down his cheeks, when I hear Borges's husky voice delivering and at once savouring the glorious lines,

[9]

Le dijo Cruz que mirara
Las últimas poblaciones
Y a Fierro dos lagrimones
Le rodaron por la cara.

and my scalp still tingles.

Read *Facundo*, read the *Memorias de Provincia*, read *Martín Fierro*, there's nothing difficult about them, Borges urged me at every turn. In time I was free to do so, and during the past five or six years, while working to compile three different collections of contemporary Argentine writing, such reading even became obligatory. For in literature, as in so much else, to understand the Argentine present (this holds true to an extent that it does not in either present-day British or American writing) one has to understand its nineteenth-century past.

A hundred and fifty years ago, Argentina was plunged in a bloody civil war in which the caudillo Juan Manuel de Rosas engaged the nation in state terror. Rosas' instrument was an organization known as the *mazorca*. Of this terror an American resident reported: 'I have seen guards at mid-day enter the houses of citizens and either destroy or bear off the furniture, turning the families into the streets, and committing other acts of violence too horrible to mention.' In the marketplace, he continued, 'Rosas hung the bodies of his many victims; sometimes decorating them, in mockery, with ribands of the Unitarian blue and even attaching to the corpses labels, on which were inscribed the revolting words "Beef with the hide." '

A decade and a half ago, Argentina was plunged in a bloody civil war in which the military caudillo Jorge Videla and his ilk engaged the nation in state terror. Videla's instrument was the armed forces. Of this terror a father reported: '. . . several men entered the building where my daughter lived, broke down her door, and forced their way in. Others stayed outside to keep watch. This episode was witnessed from the flat opposite . . . They ransacked the flat and stole possessions, then took away Selma and a friend of hers, Inés Nocetti, neither of whom has been heard from since.' The authorities labelled these victims 'materialists and atheists', 'traitors to the fatherland', 'enemies of Christian values'.

How rich in paradoxes, symmetries, and unexpected turns is the history of Argentina and the history of its literature. That in its earliest pages 150 or so years ago it should have been a literature of commitment – 'written on a drum-head . . . or between the flashes of cannon fire', as one critic put it – with a whole generation of intellectuals silenced or menaced or driven into exile, seems somehow too contemporary. While now, when we remember the year 1976 and the subsequent fates of Haroldo Conti and Rodolfo Walsh, who were murdered by the latter-day *mazorca*, and the scores of their fellow-writers who were forced to flee the country (five of them have stories in the present volume), those recent events seem quite unbelievable.

Hand in Hand Alongside the Tracks, it is hoped, follows on smoothly from where its predecessor *Celeste Goes Dancing* left off three years ago. This new selection of eighteen stories was in fact started before the earlier collection was completed, so that the same principles that guided the making of the one also hold true for the other. The only point that these samplers set out to prove is that the Argentine short story today – the genre the country's writers have come to be best at – is richly varied and accomplished.

Last time only living authors were admitted; now Humberto Costantini, who died in 1987, is represented in homage both to his achievements and to our long-standing friendship. His story, written in Mexican exile, not only falls squarely within an old Argentine tradition – the periodic banishment of intellectuals – but is also refreshing for having been written as a piece of what is known in Argentina as *literatura fantástica*.

In this collection, as in the last, variety has been a prime concern, and again, wherever possible, precedence was given recent work. While preparing the book it was my good fortune to have been able to visit Buenos Aires on four different occasions, which gave me the chance to meet new writers, especially younger ones, as well as to gather plenty of fresh material. At one point, several of them even lavished on me whole books of unpublished short stories. Along the way, once material was chosen, I was able to consult most of the writers and in the cases of the many who know English to show them drafts of the translations. That is always the translator's greatest luxury, and it obviously lightened Susan Ashe's and my burden. At the time the final selection was made, eight stories had not yet appeared in their original Spanish. Of the eighteen writers represented here, thirteen are making their initial appearance in Britain and eight their début in English anywhere.

Juan Forn has said that he and Rodrigo Fresán belong to the first Argentine generation to have been brought up entirely in the age of television. They are certainly of their time and deeply immersed in the international rock and pop culture scene. Influence from abroad shows in them. It is significant that, together with Alejandro Manara, they are fluent English-speakers and widely read in contemporary British and American fiction.

Are these signs and portents to cause worry? Time will tell. Argentines have always been notorious magpies, bringing back bits and pieces of foreign culture for their own enrichment and enlightenment. Domingo F. Sarmiento, the author of *Facundo*, the first truly Argentine book (written, of course, in exile and never published in his native land in his own lifetime), ransacked the United States for ideas about education and even imported American schoolmistresses to put those ideas into action. In our own century, literature knows no greater magpie than Jorge Luis Borges.

Argentine literature boasts many oddities. One of its

greatest practitioners, one of the country's finest observers, was William Henry Hudson, all of whose books were written in English.

Norman Thomas di Giovanni
11 December 1991

NATIONAL SOVEREIGNTY

Rodrigo Fresán

> Rented a tent, a tent, a tent;
> Rented a tent, a tent, a tent.
> Rented a tent!
> Rented a tent!
> Rented a, rented a tent.
>
> Kurt Vonnegut, Jr.
> *The Sirens of Titan*

Yesterday afternoon I saw my first Gurkha. He was squatting in front of a small fire which somehow he managed to keep alight in the drizzle. He was smiling into the void and wiping his dagger with the same tired devotion of a mother changing her baby's nappies.

I had split off from my group almost without realizing it. My idea was to look for a quiet place where I could write a letter that wasn't going anywhere in particular. We wrote a lot of them during that time. Looking like statues bent over sheets of paper, we crouched with our backs to the wind, gripping pencils in clenched fists to keep the individual letters from flying off the page. We composed our missives in the full knowledge that nobody was going to read them, because – this is a fact – the mail just wasn't that efficient. What we did was write them and read them aloud to ourselves. In this way, by turning ourselves into girl friends and families and friends, we no longer felt we were writing in vain. Sergeant Rendido let us have an hour a day for forgetting ourselves in, and that's how we hit upon this exercise of dubious worth.

Yesterday, however, I longed to be all by myself, because I was going to write the most pointless letter of all. As I was going to write to London, I had no desire to read my letter aloud. Better not. Some nutter like that freak who's forever mending his uniform might think I was a traitor. London's where my elder brother is. He works in a restaurant, and I can't help wondering what he's doing in a London restaurant. But really it's no great mystery. I suppose the idea, as ever, was to send him far away. My elder brother is said to be maladjusted. Anyway, London's where he is now. And I'm here. And I was writing to him when I saw my first Gurkha.

We used to talk about the Gurkhas all the time but until then none of us had come across one and – this may sound daft – my first thought was to ask him for his autograph. But at once I was overwhelmed by fear. The Gurkhas sliced off ears – so everyone said. The thing is, I just stood there clutching my head. The Gurkha came bounding over to me. He moved without a single wasted motion, and to my astonishment he opened his mouth and spoke to me in flawless English.

'What's up, doc?' he said in a Bugs Bunny voice.

I let out a long sigh, thinking, Right, then, this is a nightmare, and I'm going to wake up at any moment. A Gurkha imitating Bugs Bunny is more impossible and ridiculous than all the rest of this war put together.

No way. I opened and shut my eyes and opened them again, and there was the neat smile of Bugs Gurkha. He asked if I spoke English, and I said one side of my family was English.

'Really?' he said. 'Actually, that's very funny.'

He took out a packet of cigarettes and offered me one. We smoked in silence.

'And how's everything going with you lot?' he asked after a minute or two.

I said I wasn't sure what he meant by 'you lot'.

'You lot.' He made a vague gesture that might well have included the rest of the world. 'You know.'

'All right, I suppose,' I said so as not to provoke him. I was carrying my rifle on my shoulder, and the Gurkha – from what I could gather – was carrying no more than his kukri. But I'd pulled the trigger barely a couple of times in training, while the Gurkha, as he spoke, juggled with his knife as if it were an extension of his arm. I dropped my weapon and once more put my hands on my head. It was all over. I'd be taken prisoner. I remembered the Rolling Stones fan back at camp in the port. Pity he's not here, I thought.

The Gurkha blinked a few times, as if he didn't understand, and suddenly he burst out laughing. He seemed to laugh in ideograms painted in Indian ink.

'You don't understand, you don't understand,' he kept saying, holding his stomach. And when he tried to explain, again came his belly laugh. I felt I was being dreamed by someone else, a total stranger.

'I am *your* prisoner,' he finally said as he gave me his kukri, handle first.

I said, 'No, no way, I'm the one who's the prisoner.'

He kept shaking his head, moving it from side to side with the vehemence of someone who'd refused to eat his soup throughout his entire childhood.

'I-AM-YOUR-PRISONER,' he repeated, enunciating the words in capital letters and striking his breast with the palm of his hand.

I tried to make him see that it wasn't a good idea. If I took him prisoner one of those disasters that was always happening to me might happen to him. I told him it was no accident that I was wandering about the front line all alone. Nobody wanted anything to do with me. That's why the best thing was for him to take me prisoner, turn me over to his superiors, and have them lock me up in a sealed room aboard one of their warships. Or the *QE II*. They had plenty of room. And I needed a place like that to be able to think in peace.

[17]

After all, I said in conclusion, I had surrendered first. The Geneva Convention was on my side.

'No, friend, the fact that I'm a Gurkha does not mean I have to be superstitious – that's all right for worshippers of the goddess Kali. I'm your prisoner. So let's be off. Which way's your camp?'

Right, I told him, he didn't have to take me prisoner but he'd better push off fast, because it wouldn't be good for him to hang around me for long. I said I was jinxed and that I jinxed others. But it was no good.

'Prisoner am I,' he said, as if changing the word order might convince me.

That was when he bent over to pick up my rifle and hand it to me, and that was when the rifle went off. Naturally.

Fact is, I thought all these little Gurkhas were half pints. I don't know, do I? The Chinese are all small. But this one come right up to my nose. Could be they stretch a bit when they're dead, know what I mean? They brought the little geezer in day before yesterday. Poor sod. He may be the enemy and all but nobody deserves to snuff it like that. A bullet hole right between the eyes. Who'd of thought that plonker Alejo, with his luck, was such a crack shot? Or so gutsy. Thing is this war's over for both of them. The little Gurkha six foot under and Alejo in hospital and from hospital straight home. That's how it goes – some live and others die. It's only rock 'n' roll but I like it. Seems like the Gurkha jumped Alejo from behind. The little guy come wriggling along like a snake and stuck his knife in Alejo's arm. The two of them went into a clinch, then Alejo broke away, aimed, and *bang!* Paint it black, that's the way it goes, man. That Gurkha come a long way to die. And they showed him off in front of the whole camp like he was the body of Brian Jones.

So here we are at war. Who'd of thought it? Me at war. Not only that, a volunteer. Some of the lads look at me like I was nuts. But it's all part of my plan, isn't it? Thing is, I

[18]

can't tell nobody why I joined up. I got to come on the gung-ho type, *high in the sky, behind your bank of fog*, know what I mean? Because if Rendido finds out, the shit's going to hit the fan. Rendido is Sergeant Rendido. Poor bugger, thinks he's such a hawk, and stuck with a name like that – Sergeant Surrender. Rendido's more or less in charge of us. I say more or less because no one round here has a fucking clue what's going on. There are days when they all seem stoned, and, shit, don't I half miss the grass! I can't get no – *ta na na, na na na na* – I can't get no satisfaction, no satisfaction.

Miss the grass almost as much as I miss Susana. I'd miss it more if on our last night Susana hadn't finally spread her legs for me. Fact is, the redhead was terrific. After all that crap about her being a virgin and that's why she didn't want it. But following the outbreak of hostilities, like they say round here, all her shit about virginity sounded dead phony to me. That don't matter. She's under my thumb now.

She'll freak out when she gets my first letter from London. Because here's my plan: soon as we go out on patrol and things get rough, I'll make for the sidelines, shoot myself in the foot, and surrender. Ever so nice and easy, man. I'll say to them in English, Make love not war and you can round me up. The idea is they take me prisoner to London, where I sit out this war thing, and then yeah, I'll go to a Stones concert and it'll be far out, man. Couldn't let a chance like this slip through my fingers. How else would I ever see Mick and Keith in the flesh? And I swear, after the encores I'll head backstage and won't stop until I speak to Keith. See if they'll give me a job on the side, like. From watching my old man I know a thing or two about electronics. Imagine being a roadie for the Stones. That's why I said to myself let's do it – Malvinas Islands, our little lost sister, here I come! Real cool, man. It's fucking bitter, but it could be worse. Rendido gives you a lot less aggro than any of them heavies who beat the shit out of me in boot camp last year.

Ooh, they're taking the Gurkha away. I'm going to see if

I can have my picture taken with the stiff and send it to Susana.

Miss you, baby.

You can't always get what you want; you can't always get what you want; no, you can't always get what you want – but if you try sometime you just might find you get what you need.

By the time she and that bastard are found I'm going to be famous. I'm going to be a hero. That's why I'm easy about the whole thing. I'm almost not even thinking about it. There isn't much time to think anyway. We are here reclaiming what's legitimately ours, and the enemy isn't going to budge us.

Our flag's never been taken by any foe. And we are the sons of our country's founding fathers. We can't let them down.

The problem is that not everybody thinks like me. The problem is the human element. Many of the officers thought this was going to be a pushover. They never thought the enemy would send their fleet.

Wrong.

A real soldier should always think he's going to lose, analyze the causes of his hypothetical defeat, and then cross them off one by one, like someone snuffing candles with his fingertips. Without getting burnt.

But I'm speaking for myself; unfortunately I can't speak for others. And the others are almost everybody else. There they are, playing football in the rain. They fall in the mud, bang into each other, filthy as pigs, their uniforms a mess. Their uniforms aren't important to them. They even laugh at me. They laugh at how I look after my uniform, how I sew on the buttons and mend the holes. A uniform is a soldier's skin. The others can't understand this. They have no concept of heroism.

And I'm going to be a hero. By the time they find their bodies I'll be famous, and who's going to care about a little matter like that after all I'll have done for my beloved country, for my motherland? I wonder if they've been found by now, but I don't think about it as much as I did. With each day that passes I think less about them and more about myself.

That's the way it should be. Because Armageddon's getting closer. I dreamed of Armageddon again yesterday. Actually, at first I was dreaming about the two of them. I saw them on that filthy mattress, locked in each other's arms, then the shots got mixed up with the firing of Armageddon, and I saw myself running through the snow. My arm raised, I led my platoon to final victory – that victory from which one comes back a different person. Because the act of conquering is what separates gods from mortals.

I saw myself as a god. Wearing a uniform worthy of a god.

All my bullets found their mark, and the enemy's death was a beautiful thing for them, for it wasn't their death but part of my life and my glory. I watched them fall, feeling them die with a father's pride, because they'd all been born for me to kill. They'd been born so far away and had come to the ends of the earth so that, in their last living act, I would give true meaning to their lives.

I woke up excited and masturbated thinking about whether they'd been found. Bastards. They didn't even have time to get dressed. I shut the door of that shitty little flat and went straight from there to my regiment and from my regiment to the waiting planes. It was a shame I had to throw away my revolver. It had belonged to my grandfather.

The rain beat against the sandbags. Our foxholes were filling with water. I woke up several of the others but they paid no attention to me. They go on sleeping, soaked through like fish rotting in the mud. I went to Sergeant Rendido about it. He told me to stop being a ballbreaker and go back to sleep, we'd fix everything up in the morning.

I'm outside my foxhole, wrapped in my cape, eyes shut tight. I was trying to get back into my dream of Armageddon.

I've been dreaming of Armageddon ever since I can

remember. Since I was five or so. Up till now I've dreamed about a different Armageddon. With different uniforms. Like in films and television mini-series. My comrades had foreign names, and that bothered me a little, even though they were better soldiers than our side. But I think I'm better off with the new Armageddon. I am the best; yesterday a colonel came along and singled me out as an example. My uniform's impeccable. It's better now than when they gave it to me.

I have a needle and cotton.

I'm the best marksman in the platoon.

Yesterday I broke all the bottles.

Ten bottles.

Ten bullets.

You mustn't waste ammunition.

Same as I didn't on those two bastards. At this point, I imagine they must be stinking up the whole building. No, surely by now they will have found them. But they won't connect me with any of that. It will never enter their heads to pin it on me. I was very careful. Everything clean and shiny. Not a trace of blood.

Like with my uniform for Armageddon.

I go back to dreaming about Armageddon but it isn't the same. This Armageddon has serious flaws. I'm asleep but I know at once it's a dream. So much of it's implausible. The guy who killed the Gurkha's in it and that other guy too, the one who never stopped talking about the Rolling Stones, the one Rendido ordered staked out for stealing chocolate. He sang at the top of his voice all night. In English. When we untied him the next morning he didn't recognize any of us. His teeth were chattering, and he kept on calling me Keith Richards. His feet had gone all purple. Apparently they had to be amputated. Seeing's believing, and I didn't see it. Anyway, that's how they punished thieves in the old days. We never saw him again. That's why this version of Armageddon annoyed me a little. The thief was running alongside me and never stopped singing in English. I yelled at him to shut up, and all at once he was telling those two bastards, Inés and

Pedro, to shut up, since it was pointless to ask me to forgive them.

'Forgive me,' said Inés, the bitch, naked.

'Calm down.' Pedro smiled at me. It took him a while to realize that the calm down and the little smile weren't going to be enough. Then he tried to explain. He told me she'd phoned to say I was being sent to the Malvinas and she was so sad and why didn't she come by and have coffee with him. 'I swear it was her idea,' he said.

Inés laid into Pedro, cursing him like a madwoman. And there I was, sitting with the revolver in my hand, nodding and shaking my head, rubbing it against the wall. I love doing that. I have a brush cut that sticks straight up. It feels great, and they scream and scream, blaming each other.

Then Rendido wakes me with a kick. He staggers because he's drunk. He's having a hard time keeping his balance and he looks at me the way you look at somebody important, at history in the making.

'We're winning,' Rendido tells me.

Vengeance is mine, saith the Lord.

IN THE NIGHT

Humberto Costantini

Decisively, nonchalantly, the man passes through the market's main entrance. It is an imposing entrance with monumental arches and an accordion gate. The gate, he notes, is half open. The man will walk the length of the market and will try to leave by a gate at the rear. He considers (he knows) that this is a good move.

It is nearly nine o'clock, and the market is about to close. The vast, high-ceilinged hall is almost empty. The man is inside now, having walked through a big tiled vestibule with a flower stall that's shut and a blackboard with prices and a NO SPITTING sign and a smell of vinegar, spices, and cheese. Although he's walking at a good pace, the man is still only at one end of the huge hall. In the distance, near a fish stall at the far side, he sees a porter sweeping up.

Nearer to him, he sees an old woman moving towards the exit, a bundle on her back. Stooped, dressed in black, she shuffles along, eyes on the floor. The closer she comes, the more pity and revulsion the man feels.

Just before they meet, the old woman grips her heavy bundle and, with one surprisingly agile heave, lifts it onto her head. The bundle is a big piece of sackcloth knotted at the corners and filled with vegetable scraps. She now walks with the load balanced on her head, her arms held out from her sides, her neck erect, her gait dignified. Watching her, the man sees that she is not as old as he first thought. She's not old at all. She's a mature, blowsy, delectable woman, and the man

[24]

is reminded of the Italian washerwomen who used to pass his house when he was a boy.

He continues on his way and sees a butcher (he hadn't noticed him before), scrubbed, nattily turned out, standing alongside his cash register. The butcher shouts something to the night watchman, who is out of sight, and in the vast empty hall the words reverberate eerily. Distorted or muffled by repeated echoes, the voice is barely comprehensible.

Moving more quickly now, the man passes the butcher and, recognizing his face, lifts his chin in greeting. 'All right?' he says without slowing his step. 'Evening,' answers the butcher, and the man thinks he sees a look of surprise on the butcher's apple-cheeked, talcumed, fresh-out-of-the-barber's-chair face.

The man wonders whether the butcher suspects anything and decides it's unlikely, out of the question. Just to suggest these possibilities to himself has a calming effect on him.

The porter is out of sight now inside the fishmonger's stall. He reappears dragging a heavy dustbin over to his hand trolley. Just then the man hears the butcher's footsteps retreating in the direction of the main entrance. He hears someone (the night watchman) whistling a tango in the urinals.

The man knows there is a cold, grimy, ill-lit passage at the end of the hall. Down a few steps, through the passage, up again, and you come to an earthen-floored courtyard and beyond it the market's rear exit.

The passage runs between the urinals and the cold-storage lockers. The man feels cold here, even colder than out on the street, where it was cold enough. The place stinks of toilets, ammonia, fish, meat, rotten apples, disinfectant, and damp – all at once and one after another.

A single forty-watt light bulb, encrusted with filth, dangles from a wire and lights just enough of the passage for the man to see broken and missing floor tiles, a pile of feathers, a bundle of sacks, a blood-soaked crate, a number of dustbins. He crosses this stretch with comparative ease only to come upon a swing door that serves no purpose. On the other side of it, the corridor is in complete darkness. Considering it unwise to prop the door open to let in the dim light, the man feels his way carefully along the walls, his left hand touching the cold-storage rooms, his right the doors of the toilets.

After the short ascent at the end of the passage, the man knows he'll find a solid iron door with an outsize bolt and padlock. Through the door, he knows, lies the market's rear courtyard, a tangle of weeds, mud, odds and ends, and litter. And at the far end of this yard, the door out onto the street. This is what the man is looking for.

He gropes his way up the three steps. There's the iron door. He slides back the bolt, which is as thick as a broom handle, and opens the door. So far so good, the man tells himself.

He slips silently through the door out into the open. The night sky is overcast, starless. Not even the street lamp, which he reckons is somewhere nearby, manages to shed any light here. This seems strange, but he thinks that some tree must be hiding it, or that there has been a sudden power cut, or that the lamp isn't working – that stones have been flung at it. He moves cautiously.

The man remembers (or thinks he remembers) every detail of this yard. Among the caked mud and weeds is a narrow concrete path. This path, a makeshift track for hand trolleys, curves to the right, skirting a tap, then continues in a straight line to the door.

The thing is to stick to the path, the man thinks to himself, so as to avoid tripping over some crate or stepping in the soft ground around the tap, which, forever dripping, forms a stinking puddle strewn with rotten vegetables, bits of paper, feathers, broken glass, and plastic containers.

This path, the man thinks, can't be more than ten or fifteen yards long. Then the door and the street – his street – a hundred and fifty yards from his house.

Only at the last minute had it occurred to him to cross through the market to reach his destination rather than to use the side street. As the taxi carrying him from the airport turned into the avenue a few blocks from his house, he had suddenly said to the driver, 'Here at the corner,' and got out. Luckily he wasn't encumbered with luggage.

Of his flight – how strange – the man remembers very little. I must have gone out like a light straight after take-off, he says to himself. Yes, all that last minute fuss and rushing about. He has a hazy memory of stopovers in Caracas and Lima. At neither of them did he leave his seat.

Quite clear in his mind, however, was the reason for his trip. The man feels an overwhelming wave of emotion when he thinks of seeing them, hugging and kissing them, protecting them, being with them again. But not even in his thoughts dare he mention their names, and he's glad about this. It shows that his instinct for self-preservation is functioning.

This memory and his emotions cause a lapse in his concentration, and he walks into something. Groping, he can feel that it is a chicken coop, one side smashed in, which someone has left in the way. He steps round it into the weeds and then is back on the path. He treads on something squishy – feathers? a toad? chicken guts? Now he proceeds towards the door more warily.

The man remembers that door, a single rickety, noisy sheet of rusty metal reinforced with iron rods. Over the top of the door is a row of vertical bars, and above that (for some unknown reason) a sort of small pitched roof made of zinc.

His hand touches an unplastered wall. The door, he reckons, must be to his right. Picking his way gingerly among the weeds, he runs a hand over the wall from left to right, feeling the bricks, the mortared joints, holes with spiders' nests in them, a small wild-tobacco plant, a buttress. He goes back over everything again in the opposite direction. There is no door.

'Shit!' the man murmurs foolishly. They must have bricked it up. And he dithers before deciding that it could be risky to jump the wall at this time of night. Riskier even than taking the side street.

Meanwhile, he must retrace his steps all the way back through the market and out of the main door onto the avenue.

Now that he has done it once, he estimates that the whole thing cannot take him more than six or seven minutes. From the avenue he will work out how to get home.

The concrete path again, his eyes are used to the dark or else light is filtering in from somewhere, because he can make out the way. What he had stepped on, he sees now, were chicken innards wrapped in a sheet of the *Crónica*.

In less time than he had calculated, he reaches the iron door. It's shut. The man thinks he remembers leaving it open. He tries the handle. Hopeless. Before knocking off, the watchman must have locked it. The man peers through a chink but cannot see any light. He dismisses the idea of banging to wake up the watchman. He hesitates. Should the watchman suspect him of anything, it could cause problems. These days, watchmen and janitors . . .

Trapped here in this courtyard, then, the only way out is over the wall. But it is still too early for that. Perhaps he should wait a while longer.

Back he goes along the concrete path, which he can now see quite clearly. The light, he has just noticed, is coming from the open transom of an adjoining house. He won't jump until the light goes out. Meanwhile, it will allow him to study the wall. He wants to size up its height, find out if it is topped with broken glass or barbed wire, and locate a foothold. This time, combing the length of wall, he comes across something he had not spotted before. Where the door should have been, he finds a thick, vertical strip of metal embedded in the brickwork, and roughly welded to this strip three or four feet up from the ground is a sort of heavy wrought-iron handle which shows signs of use.

He cannot quite work out what it's all for, but instinctively he grips the handle and wrenches it towards him. The wall is falling in on him. At least, damn it, that is the feeling he gets.

The whole surface of the old sheet-iron door, he discovers, has been built out with bricks inside an iron frame. This patchwork strikes the man as rather odd, but immediately he tries to explain it away. It is to make the door heavier, he thinks, or to stop its squeaking, or to keep dogs out. Though, as a matter of fact, he no longer much cares. Tugging on the handle, he has opened the door a crack, and now, in the middle of the wall, he sees the door's outline, half-hidden by the tall weeds.

He tugs again, eagerly, and finds the crack widening bit by bit. He keeps pulling until he thinks he can squeeze through. With his shoulders, hands, and a hip he applies force, and all at once he finds himself on the street.

The man takes a deep breath, brushes himself off, looks at his watch. Twenty-five to ten. It is a freezing, windy winter's night, and along the whole block there is not a soul in sight. He hasn't been spotted. Turning, he carefully pulls the brick door shut.

He steps up to the kerb to scan the next block – their block, he thinks, the one where their house is. This street seems less deserted. He sees several parked vehicles. He also sees a neighbour – whom he knows – head down, hands in his pockets, running across the road under a street lamp and disappearing indoors. At the same time he sees a woman in a dark coat with a green scarf tied round her head. She comes towards him and, on reaching the corner, turns in the direction of the avenue. Nothing odd in that, he thinks.

Although he keeps repeating to himself, Nothing odd in that, nothing odd in that, as he walks along the man begins to feel jumpy. Approaching the block, he turns his attention to the vehicles, counting them. There are nine, four on the left, five on the right, all facing his way. It is a one-way street, which makes surveillance easy.

He puts on a nonchalant expression, feigns a yawn, and crosses the street at the corner. To his annoyance, the man realizes he has made a mistake. He should have skirted the street lamp. But it's done now, he thinks, and too late to go back.

He is half-way across the street (naively, his lips are pursed to whistle) when he makes out two heads in the third car on the right. A couple, he tells himself.

With a thrill, he once again surveys his own neighbourhood, his own street. Opposite him stand the grocer's shop, closed (as usual) and completely abandoned, the three blocks of flats, the cigarette kiosk, its sign, the shadow of its sign dancing eerily against the wall.

On his side, between two tall buildings that hem it in, he sees the old house on the corner, its chain-link fence, its tiny garden, its dog, and that girl, whose name he struggles to remember. Faustina, he says to himself, then, No, no, Paulina. And it cheers him to have remembered. He sees Paulina with her long plaits, the gold studs in her ears, her school pinafore, and her smile. She is washing clothes in the patio sink.

Unawares, he has left the side street behind, stepped up onto the kerb, and is now on familiar ground. This is his pavement, the man thinks, the pavement leading to his house. Lifting his eyes, he notices across the street towards the end of the block a figure leaning against the wall. This is the exact spot where a tree casts a shadow.

The man feels (relives, feels again) his old, familiar fear. A vague, lurking, permanent fear. Perhaps it is just being back in the city, the man thinks. In fact, he cannot explain why he has not felt this fear before. Why now?

The fear sharpens his senses. It's not a couple in the car but three or four men. His sixth sense tells him they are watching him.

The figure by the wall comes towards him and stops in the shadow of the next tree. There is a movement inside the car. Thirty yards, the man thinks, and he will be home. With them, he says to himself. And then, in a flash, comes the sudden conviction that *they will not be there*. But that would be utterly absurd, he thinks. How stupid of me. What made me think that? He is on the verge of declaring himself an idiot, an arse-hole, before he realizes (is convinced) that the men in the car (he no longer has the least doubt who they are) are waiting for him.

He believes he still has time. This is the ideal moment to

double back and vanish – preferably at a run. What made me think they won't be there? he wonders again, automatically drawing back against the wall. He turns round.

At this point he sees another car, a grey Ford Falcon with three men inside. The car has just passed the house on the corner and is now heading down the one-way street the wrong way. The man watches the car advancing slowly towards him.

'Shit, I'm trapped,' the man mutters. 'I've had it. I shan't get out of this one.' And he swears. He cannot work out how he has managed to get himself into this jam. Nothing, not even a .22, between me and handing myself over, he thinks, and he is scared out of his wits. He glances desperately from side to side. It's clear there's no way out.

Two men step from the parked car, one carrying a .45 and the other a Fal. Through the car window, he can clearly make out the glistening barrel of an Ithaka pointing his way.

The figure by the wall purposefully crosses the road. The Ford Falcon comes to a stop some ten yards away. It's partly hidden by a van, but voices can be heard from it and the sound of doors slamming.

Where can they be? What will they be like? the man wonders. I hope they won't torture me for long, I hope they kill me straightaway. He sees his body thrown face down in among weeds, mud, and spent cartridges. And he sees his mutilated face, his bound wrists, and the pool of blood.

He's choking. He's also hot. He also feels cramps in his stomach. He feels the cold sweat on the back of his neck. 'So this is this,' he mumbles in utter confusion. What he means is, So this is what death is like.

He sees them ringing him in, closer and closer, the two armed men, the one by the wall, and the three who got out of the Falcon. The one with the pistol cries out, 'Hold it!' and speaks his name clearly. I've had it now, the man thinks. And to his surprise, the certainty wipes away his fear.

While the man with the Fal points it at his belly, and one of the men from the Falcon takes something out of his jacket

pocket, the man struggles impotently and feverishly to understand how it could have come to this. How could he have let
himself be trapped in such a stupid way?

In a split second, as if his salvation depended on it, he tries
to review the steps (the chain of circumstances) which have
brought him so absurdly to this final one.

As if on speeded-up film, each inexplicable, incomprehensible step of only a few minutes ago rushes before his eyes.
Everything – the market, the half-open gate, the woman with
the bundle on her head, the butcher, the grimy passageway,
the door with the padlock, the brickwork door, and then
the freezing night, the street corner under the lamp, his
neighbourhood, the empty grocer's, the kiosk, Paulina's house
between the two tall buildings, the four vehicles on the left
and the five on the right, the man leaning against the wall, the
Falcon behind him, his name on the lips of the fellow with
the gun – everything, everything, he feels, is linked (was
linking up) so as to shape this perfect, silent, ineluctable trap
now tightening relentlessly round him.

While the man with the pistol barks out orders, and the
man with the Ithaka gets out of the car, taking aim, and the
ones in the Falcon make a rush at him, the man thinks he sees
(makes an effort to see) that in this apparently perfect,
apparently ineluctable trap something – one part, one small
piece – does not quite fit, does not click into place like the
other pieces.

And impelled by the danger, almost caught in the jaws of
the trap, the man keeps wondering what this small piece – this
faulty piece that will not fit – can be. Only by means of it
might he still effect an escape.

Speedily, dizzily, with the doggedness of a caged animal,
he goes over and over every element of the trap: the market,
the gate, the woman . . .

He feels giddy. What he is doing seems idiotic. He tells
himself that it would be more sensible to prepare for a
dignified end. He rests his head against the wall, relaxing, and
in that moment – to his amazement, desperate to believe what

he thinks he has found out – it dawns on him what the tiny flawed piece, the piece that does not fit, is.

This piece, then, is his one hope, however faint. And it is through it, through the hairsbreadth that this ill-fitting piece leaves, that he may still just possibly escape.

The market, the gate, the woman . . . Got it, the man thinks, trying to convince himself. The bogus piece must be Paulina's house. It must be Paulina and her plaits and her gold stud earrings and her patio sink. Here's where he may be able to get away.

For everything is, everything seems to be, horrifyingly real. Only Paulina did not exist. Paulina's house could not have existed. On that corner, he now thinks he remembers, there is a big block of flats. The street corner he saw as he was crossing the road is (was) the street corner of thirty years ago. This is the flawed piece, the bit that does not work.

And he tries to force this piece to mesh with the apparently well-fitting, apparently perfect mechanism of the trap: the butcher's meaningless words, the crone who later turned into an appetizing woman, the outlandish brick door . . .

He begins to suspect that everything he is going through is a dream. To prove it, to convince himself that the guns pointed at him and the men grabbing him by the lapels are only part of this horrible dream (as two of these quasi-policemen pin his arms, and another with the skill of a prizefighter gives him a jab in the gut, and someone from behind covers his eyes and mouth with a kind of scarf or blindfold), the man makes a tremendous, almost superhuman, effort of will and says aloud, 'It's all a dream.' And at once, the sound of his own voice wakes him.

There's a pain in his chest, he has difficulty breathing, his pillow is wet. He fumbles for the switch, turns on the bedside lamp, and looks round. After a moment or two, he lights a cigarette, his hand still shaky. Perhaps I'll have a letter from them this week, he says to himself, even now, as he slowly exhales, not daring to utter his children's names. Slowly the smoke rises to the whitewashed ceiling of his small room in

Colonia Anzures, a suburb of Mexico City, over five thousand miles from Buenos Aires.

He hears the first lorry rattling down the street. The man knows that in a little while it will be dawn.

PALISAVA
Elvira Orphée

At that time I wasn't old. I lived with my husband in the country where he came from. Here, in the place we live now, his people are called Turks but they aren't Turks. My daughter Palisava was growing up then, and, because she was so sweet and beautiful and bursting with health, no one could help staring at her. She had chestnut hair and big eyes that made you wonder whether sleep of any kind could ever completely close them. Only a long sleep might, a sleep as high as flying.

One holiday my husband and I went out for a stroll in the streets. Seeing us from a house that belonged to someone we didn't know, Palisava ran out, looking so sweet.

'Mummy,' she said, 'tomorrow I have to go before the Tribunal to die.'

When you are on the verge of tears, nothing is clear. I asked Palisava why she had to die – as if there could be any reason for it, mine or the world's. I had nothing but despair; as for the world, Palisava was its ornament.

'It's tomorrow,' she said. 'I must die tomorrow because I don't believe what they believe.'

I begged her to let me go in her place. By then, my heart but not my eyes was full of tears. We'd both die, she said. As women it was not for us to think or have beliefs but only to obey. We should not feel that the Tribunal or those who ordered us not to think were evil.

I'm a poor simple woman. I never understood what made

the Tribunal like God, who sees everything. Since they hadn't carted my daughter off but were leaving her to give herself up, I didn't understand why she couldn't run away. I looked at my husband, hoping that he might say, 'I'll go in her place. I'm a man; I wear no veil over my face. I have the right to defend myself.' He said nothing but only looked away, vaguely, tenderly.

Palisava put her arms round me. 'I'll come back, mummy. Don't throw away any of my things. When I'm back we shall be so close you won't know whether I am there before your very eyes or inside you.'

I looked at her little violet chemise. I thought of all her little chemises, of the little sandals she wore with socks to keep out the cold and dust. Afterwards, for a long time, I thought about nothing. Even my memories had vanished, washed away by the tears I wept in my heart.

And all the time I wasn't remembering, my husband and I lived somewhere else — in a country with a seaside and pink houses. How did he ever manage to get away from the land of his fathers, with its walls that ran in all directions? I have no idea. Maybe he made up to the Tribunal, maybe he became one of them. Maybe when they saw the vague, tender expression on his face they could tell he was neither raging nor weeping, and they didn't consider a man like him worth killing.

I think it was in that country beside the sea, where we had gone to live, that my memories began to come back. My husband, who up until that time had been a grown man, became a boy again. And I almost a girl. I say almost, because even very young mothers seem older than their husbands. They have more on their minds.

One day, sitting on a wall, my husband playfully poked at something on the ground with his foot. It turned out to be a pair of tiny green snakes. They were very short and thin and a brilliant, almost transparent, green. He played with them quite unafraid.

At that point my memory was still unclear. I thought

[36]

Palisava was with us in those years, a little girl with short hair in loose curls but really she had already died, a big girl with long hair. I pictured her as little, then all at once I did not picture her at all. My memory is now so bad that I no longer know whether we came to this country with the pink houses before or after she died. I think it was after, because my husband was playing with the little snakes and he called them Palisava. Would he have called them that if she had been there with us? Even if she had not been with us, it was wrong of him to call creatures like them by our beloved daughter's name. But for some reason it did not upset me much.

The snakes did not seem so wicked. They showed no interest whatever in me. How could they have been Palisava, whom I loved so much and who loved me so much? My husband talked to them. I have no idea what he said. Was it wicked of him to speak to them and call them by his daughter's name? They were green, and my lovely Palisava had chestnut hair. I am a poor ignorant old woman. Was it right or was it wicked?

All this came like a flash of light in the long darkness of mourning. After that I fell back into not remembering, into blackness, into a time without memories. Maybe I too had died, and it was better. Now I'm alive again to go on suffering, perhaps worse than ever.

We came to this country and to this village, where my husband goes about selling trinkets from a little cart. I must have worked too, otherwise how would we have eaten? Perhaps the women here were very kind and helped me. Even if it has not happened to them, they feel a bond with a woman whose daughter is dead.

Then one day memories of when Palisava was alive flooded back (the later memories never returned), and it was terrible. Into the earthen courtyard of my house came a long, fierce, bright-green snake, green and hissing and very angry with me. But the creature got on with my husband and talked to him. I never heard them; I only know because he told me what the snake said. That's how I found out that it wanted to strike at me, a writhing, wriggling fury.

My husband called the snake Palisava and told me what it said. It asked for her things – Palisava's little chemises. The snake said that she'd told me she would come back and asked me to keep them but that I had thrown them away. And she had come back. That's what the snake said, but I did not believe it. How could such an evil, frightening beast be my sweet Palisava?

The snake guessed at what was passing through my mind. It knew that I was asking myself why this dirty, crawling thing needed Palisava's little socks and sandals to keep out the dust. Reading my thoughts, the creature told me through my husband that it did not want her things any more.

Why didn't I run away? As Palisava had not escaped her killers, I was not escaping now. Why? People don't run away, because until something terrible takes place no one believes it will happen to them.

All at once I remembered that I had never thrown out anything of Palisava's. I couldn't have, even during the time I had no memory. I wouldn't have parted with a single garment that had touched Palisava, not ever, because in her body was her sweet soul. Sweet and full of despair when she went to her death. Could anyone have thrown away her little chemises?

The beast did not hear me think this. Angrier than ever, it hurled itself at me. To be exact, the snake somehow got inside me, coiling all the way down my spine, for the beast was twice my size and very thick. Now it crushes my bones, making me cry out. It presses on everything inside me, the part that breathes, the part that eats, the part that sleeps. Even during the little sleep my pain allows me, I can hear Palisava's voice as she went to her death.

'I'll come back, mummy,' she says, 'and we shall be so close you won't know whether I am there before your very eyes or inside you.'

TO KILL A HARE

José Pablo Feinmann

Everyone knew that don Julio wanted a grandson – everyone in Coronel Andrade, where don Julio lived and would probably die. He was that kind of man, one with roots, and he would die on some peaceful evening, or in his bed beside his wife Elena on a moonlit, cricket-filled night, or perhaps in his ironmonger's shop, which was the biggest and best-stocked in town and where don Julio spent the best part of his time, waiting on customers, chatting with the neighbours, and keeping an eye on things: on his shop assistants, and even on Julito, who was a good lad but a bit absent-minded. Julito had been married to Fabiana for four years now, four years without a sign of anything – at any rate, without a sign of what everyone in Coronel Andrade knew don Julio wanted. A grandson.

To make matters worse, Fabiana had blossomed. Her breasts filled out her jumper, her legs were long, her hips broad, and, except when the evening wind made it stand up on end in a wild, unkempt tangle, her hair fell tidily on her shoulders. What was more, her bearing, posture, and walk all revealed a femininity that tended to upset people. 'She's a stuck-up miss,' said the town gossips as they swept their front doorsteps or went about their shopping. 'The thing is, working behind that cosmetics counter, she spends the whole day tarting herself up and primping.' It was true that Fabiana worked in a chemist's, where she earned good money. But the explanation was simpler. She had blossomed. Fabiana had become a woman – and a beautiful one.

Julito resigned himself to this transformation in his long-time betrothed. Like many other couples in Coronel Andrade, he and Fabiana became engaged so young that they no longer remembered when. Perhaps when they were nine, or even – who knew? – six or seven. Whichever, they had experienced everything together, from their earliest games to their first shy, fleeting kisses. At nineteen, they were married. Twenty-three now, Fabiana was a well-endowed woman, while Julito was still a withdrawn, melancholy, rather delicate adolescent of average height, who was as affectionate to his mother as he was obedient to and even nervous of his father. Fabiana herself, on their Sunday family visits or behind the cosmetics counter, was perfectly cheerful and fond of saying in her clear, young voice, 'Fact is, Julito's never grown properly. I'm going to have to fatten him up.'

So that's how things stood. Who would have thought it possible? Certainly not don Julio – although everyone could see that it was not Fabiana's fault, healthy and beautiful as she was, but Julito's, that the longed-for grandson never arrived.

None of this, however, prevented father and son every Sunday (at least until Alberto appeared) from indulging a passion for rough shooting – a passion that had drawn them together ever since Julito was little more than a child. This is what they did. At first light, don Julio fetched his son, who would be waiting by the door of his house, the butt of his shotgun on the pavement and his foot propped against the wall. Off they'd go into the woods, wearing knee boots, leather jackets, and woollen caps tied under the chin. Either it was too cold, or they didn't have much to say, or they were concentrating too hard on what they were doing, but they hardly spoke. From time to time, however – half joking, half serious – don Julio would repeat the advice he had given his son the very first time they had gone out. 'If you want to kill a hare,' don Julio

said, 'the main thing is to aim at the hare and not at yourself.'
The remark always had a humiliating, almost contemptuous,
ring to it. Who in his right mind would do anything else?

They would return in the middle of the day, muddy, their
hands and clothes blood-spattered. They'd go straight to don
Julio's, where the rest of the family was waiting – doña Elena,
Fabiana, cousins, uncles, aunts, grandparents. While Julito
placed the pick of the game over a ready-prepared fire, a
jubilant don Julio would say that it was of course he who had
bagged it and not Julito, who as usual had missed any number
of chances.

As the years went by, the fruitless wait for a grandson
exacerbated don Julio's taunts. For Julito, Sundays became
the saddest day of the week.

Alberto appeared one Monday. Arriving very early at the
ironmongery, he shyly – or, you might say, tentatively and
respectfully – had a word with don Julio, who was already
there, since it was he who always opened the shop. And
Alberto said to excuse his boldness but he needed work
because, on account of the owner's death, the bakery where
he had been for two years had closed down, putting him out
of a job. He had a wife, he told don Julio. He'd been married
six months, and his wife, whose name was Lucía, had been
pregnant for three of them. Don Julio listened carefully and
looked Alberto up and down. The old man liked the boy. The
frank, almost easy laugh that lit up his eyes, his strong build,
his big, bony hands – don Julio liked all of it. He asked him
his age, and Alberto told him twenty.

'And you're going to be a father so soon,' said don Julio.

'That's right, sir,' Alberto said.

Smiling in satisfaction, don Julio gave the boy an affectionate clap on the back and a job.

Alberto was good at his work, enthusiastic. But at the same
time he did nothing that might upset Julito, always giving him
his due as the owner's son. This no doubt was what made it

possible for the two young men to be friends. They became inseparable. Side by side in the sturdy old van with *Don Julio Ironmongers* on its doors, the two covered the town and surrounding countryside, making deliveries, collecting bills, and generally drumming up trade. Side by side they helped to unload the lorries that brought stock from Buenos Aires. Side by side they stayed on with don Julio until the last minute, until the till was locked up and the shutters pulled down, and, if the day's sales had been good, all three called in for an aperitif at the bar across the street. Such was the way things went in Coronel Andrade. And such was the simplicity of don Julio's life.

It must have been this sense of well-being, of all-round contentment, which one evening – another of those when he had just closed the ironmongery – made the old man invite Julito and Alberto to the best café in town. Don Julio ordered three beers. Beer with a tray of titbits. Then, when the waiter had served them, the old man lifted his glass, took a long look at each of the boys, smiled, and said, 'Here's to my two sons.' Alberto smiled. And, glancing at his father, Julito raised his glass, sipped his beer, and, as if in obedience, also smiled.

From time to time, don Julio talked about his one sorrow. He talked about it wherever he was – at the Sunday family reunions (there particularly), at the café, and even at the ironmongery. A man of his age, he would say – and he spelled it out, a man of sixty – needs a reason to go on living. That was why he wanted a grandson. That was all. Being a grandfather was different from being a father, he would go on to explain. A man had time to be a grandfather but not to be a father. A man became a father when he was young, when life ate away at him with its problems. Whereas, when he became a grandfather he was already formed and had time to enjoy a child's mischief. Everyone said don Julio was right. And they said yes, they understood, but he must be patient and someday it would happen. Then they would look at Julito

– not at Fabiana, at Julito – who by now had tried everything, including trips to Buenos Aires, innumerable visits to doctors, ridiculous and even humiliating tests. At Julito, who had reached the stage of being painfully convinced that he was never going to satisfy his father's demand.

Six months after Alberto came to work in the ironmongery, his wife Lucía had a baby that weighed close to nine pounds. He was strong and beautiful. A month later, he was baptized. Don Julio was godfather, and the child was named Julio Manuel.

The reason to go on living that don Julio needed was given him by Alberto's son. There were changes in the ironmongery. Don Julio no longer came in early. Alberto and Julito had to push themselves, to work harder, to take on responsibilities. It was not easy, but they did it. Don Julio, meanwhile, began to scale down his participation in the shop, and this became more and more obvious. He still saw suppliers, dealt with the bank, and locked the till at night. But nothing else. The rest of the day he spent with Julio Manuel, taking him for walks in the park, buying him toys, and listening for his happy little chuckle, which was as happy as Alberto's.

And it was probably the gratitude which don Julio inevitably began to feel for Alberto – while discovering, magically, each of the child's expressions in the young man's face and vice versa – that brought the two men closer and closer. It was a closeness that left Julito on the sidelines.

What was more, Alberto, his wife Lucía, and little Julio Manuel began to be invited to the Sunday family reunions. This might not have been so painful for Julito had not his father – happy face flushed with wine, hugging Alberto in hearty enthusiasm – invariably said, 'This is one hell of a lad!' And pointing to Julio Manuel, 'Look at the tiger he's brought into the world.' Hurtful as all this was, still greater humiliation lay in store for Julito.

It happened one Saturday. Don Julio, Julito, and Alberto

had been at the ironmongery all day, balancing the books. When it was almost time to close, don Julio said to his son, 'We'll have to finish this tomorrow. It won't need all three of us. You come in, Julito.' Always ready to obey his father, Julito agreed. He was not one to shirk. The blood froze in his veins, however, when, laying an affectionate hand on Alberto's shoulder, don Julio said, 'Expect me first thing in the morning. We're going out for some shooting. I know you haven't got a gun, but never mind. I'll buy you one if you make me a promise.'

'What's that, don Julio?' said Alberto.

'Hurry up and give your wife another son as beautiful as Julio Manuel.'

Very sure of himself, Alberto smiled. 'Don't worry about that,' he said.

Then and there, Julito decided to do what he had to do the following day, Sunday, as soon as don Julio and Alberto got back from shooting. Only extreme pain could have given rise to such a strange – for want of a better word – idea.

Blaming a backlog of work (responsibility for balancing the books had been dumped on him, he summoned the nerve to say), Julito arrived late at the family reunion. Everyone else was already there – grandparents, uncles and aunts, the boisterous cousins. Doña Elena stood by the grill, raking the coals. Fabiana and Lucía sat together at the table, from time to time chatting and smiling – although not much. That is, Fabiana, who this Sunday was far from showing her usual good – not to say infectious – humour, was not smiling much. She looked sad, gloomy, perhaps because of what she and Julito had talked about the night before, perhaps because it was getting more and more difficult to sit there beside Lucía, who was rocking little Julio Manuel in her arms and, with this simple but undoubtedly important act, receiving the smiles, fond looks, and good wishes – in short, the favouritism – of everyone.

[44]

They were all there except don Julio and Alberto, who showed up just before two that afternoon and were welcomed like conquering heroes, with clapping all round – clearly the product of great appetites and a demijohn of wine. Doña Elena began to prepare the game, and, pouring himself a generous glass of wine, this time don Julio confessed in his loud, imperious voice that the credit was not all his, that Alberto had turned out to be quite a shot and hardly ever missed. Then, to the cruel rejoicing of everyone, don Julio said something he perhaps shouldn't have. 'Where this young man aims his eye' – and here he raised one of Alberto's arms like a boxing champ – 'that's where he puts his bullet.' Lucía gently smiled, almost to herself, pressed little Julio Manuel to her breast, and went on rocking him. With everyone contradicting him, affectionately and admiringly, Alberto said that don Julio exaggerated, that it hadn't been quite like that. A bit apart from the rest, Fabiana and Julito sought each other's eyes. In shame, however, Julito dropped his.

They ate and drank for the rest of the day. As evening came on (during the sort of lull when one uncle or another begins to strum a guitar, some precocious cousin joins in singing, and, inevitably, a few couples stand up and start to dance), Julito approached Alberto and said he wanted to talk to him. Calm, showing no surprise, Alberto accepted.

They strolled a long way down the dirt track that skirted the back of the house. Alberto listened in silence, from time to time giving a slight nod. Only when Julito had finished did Alberto ask if Fabiana knew about what he had just suggested. Julito said yes, she did, he'd talked it over with her the night before, and she'd agreed. At that, Alberto assented. Without another word, they went back to the house.

Nobody saw, nobody knew what Julito did that night. Perhaps he went to some dive on the edge of town and drowned his sorrows in gin. It's not hard to imagine him there – sad, full of self-pity, elbows propped on a corner table. Perhaps he was at the pictures watching one of those old films that used to run in Coronel Andrade. Or perhaps he just strolled aimlessly up and down the dark, deserted streets. What is clear is that he got home late, later than ever before. He went into the bedroom, shut the door, and didn't turn on the light. Fabiana was asleep or pretending to be. Julito got in beside her and lay there, face up, his eyes wide-open in the dark.

Three months later, Fabiana told everyone she was pregnant. She announced it at one of the Sunday reunions – that's how it had to be done, in front of the whole family – proudly, very conscious of the importance of the fabulous news everyone had so long awaited. With tears in his eyes, don Julio folded his son in his arms. And they all drank to the couple's happiness and to the health of the future heir, don Julio's much-desired grandson. For, better than the son of Fabiana and Julito, the expected child just announced to the world was, of course, don Julio's grandson.

With elaborate, painstaking enthusiasm, don Julio began personally to take charge of Fabiana. Visiting her every day with little Julio Manuel, the old man flooded her with advice – she must not try to do too much, she must get a lot of sleep, she must eat well. These were happy days, days of real glory for don Julio. He spread the news to every last person in town. He told it to anyone who would listen. As well as to anyone who wouldn't. Any number of times, he declared his sudden pride in his son. And he demonstrated it. One afternoon at the ironmongery, in front of all the employees, in front of Alberto and the customers too, he gave his son a magnificent present – a double-barrelled German shotgun. 'A real jewel,' everyone said. Julito was moved; he promised to take better care of it than of his life. 'Whatever I could give you is little,' don Julio said to him. 'It's nothing beside the happiness you've given me.'

That Sunday, don Julio, Julito, and Alberto went out shooting together.

*　　*　　*

Life, needless to say, is full of surprises. Don Julio's death was a surprise. It happened in Fabiana and Julito's house on one of those afternoons when, as usual, don Julio had taken little Julio Manuel with him to visit his daughter-in-law. Suddenly he said he felt ill, dizzy, sick. That his chest hurt. Fabiana put him to bed and called the family doctor. But it was too late. Barely an hour later, don Julio, as he himself used to put it, had gone to a better life.

The wake was held that same night, and he was buried the next morning. None of them could explain, though they thought up a thousand reasons for it, why Julito did not show up at the wake or the burial.

Six months after that, almost on the very date set by the doctor, Fabiana gave birth. At the clinic, the excited, babbling family congratulated the couple but grieved that don Julio was not there to welcome his long-awaited grandson, a beautiful boy who, they said, would have brought his grandfather such happiness – particularly if you took it into account that he looked unbelievably like Julio Manuel, whom, as everyone knew, don Julio had loved so much.

Early one Sunday two weeks later, Julito went out shooting alone. He took the gun his father had given him. It was midnight when Fabiana, trembling with fear, told the family that he had not yet got back. The alarm was raised. They searched until dawn, which was when they found him in some bushes, his head blown apart and his hand curled round the magnificent double-barrelled German shotgun.

Doña Elena sold the ironmongery. Alberto stayed on to work for the new owners. And barely two months after Julito's death, Fabiana left the town with her little son, never to return.

HAND IN HAND
ONE WHOLE AFTERNOON
ALONGSIDE THE TRACKS

Sylvia Iparraguirre

On platform fourteen, the clock showed that the Olavarría
train was about to leave. Half lifted by the bearded man who
was with her, the girl scrambled up through the last door of
the last carriage. He handed her a bag, hesitated, and climbed
up after her. They looked at each other, uncomfortable,
flustered. The bearded man was the first to avert his eyes. In
one of her hands the girl carried a heavy winter jacket; in the
other, a number of books and a large folder. She was not really
a girl. Although her slender figure and the long, straight hair
that hung down over her face made her look like a slightly
scatty adolescent, she was in fact thirty. Her name was
Jorgelina.

The man gave her some hurried advice, drowned by the
noise of other voices and the train's whistle. My goodness,
thought Jorgelina, how am I going to get to carriage seventeen?

From the corridor doorway a soldier watched them indifferently.

'Please,' the bearded man said suddenly, 'could you help
her to her seat with all this?'

Without shifting, the boy nodded. His cap was tucked under
a shoulder strap. The man and Jorgelina exchanged a quick
kiss. She was always running for trains and coaches at the last
minute, but this time it was not her fault. He got down, and
she peered out of the door waving her hand for a long while.

Jorgelina turned and met the boy's eyes. He had her bag in his hand and looked as if he were ready for action. He was tall and beefy and had a boy's round face. They set off down the packed corridors, the soldier going first to clear the way. Her mind still elsewhere, Jorgelina let herself be led. He would know where carriage seventeen was; the dreary part now was the eight-hour journey before her and these first moments away from Nicolás.

They reached the compartment. Effortlessly, the soldier tossed the bag onto the luggage rack. Jorgelina heaped her things higgledy-piggledy on the seat. The boy watched as if waiting for something from her – something to do, an order – and there he'd be, the soldier, on hand but not volunteering for anything. An idea crossed Jorgelina's mind.

'Have you got a ticket?' she asked.

The boy blushed. He shook his head.

'Why don't you sit there,' she said. 'For the moment, it doesn't seem to be taken. We can fix it with the guard later on.'

Before she had finished, she regretted her words. She did not want to have to talk to the boy just because he'd helped her with her bag. Particularly since the soldier was bound to be going all the way to Olavarría or at least to Azul, which would only give her an hour on her own. There's always the dining-car, thought Jorgelina. She sat down and offered the boy a cigarette. He accepted it, grateful. When Jorgelina lit it for him she saw his hands, huge and tanned, the sides of his fingers criss-crossed with tiny black lines. The soldier leaned back in his seat; no longer shy, he seemed ready to talk. His boyish face wore a good-natured smile.

'You from Buenos Aires?' he asked.

She said yes, and suddenly she felt cheerful. There was something about the boy that she liked. 'And you?'

'I am too. I'm on my way to Azul.' He laughed. 'Obviously – where else could I be going in this uniform and on this train? I've been in for six months now.'

'You have friends at the base.' Jorgelina put it as a statement.

The boy looked at her as if she understood nothing. He said, in the tone of one explaining something to a halfwit, 'Me, I've only got one friend. I'm the stay-at-home type; I like being with my family. So if you mean best mates, I've got only one. As he's a year older, I was just going in when he was coming out. Funnily enough, he ended up at Azul too. We overlapped by one month. I was really cut up when he left.'

Jorgelina's curiosity was aroused. The boy spoke with true candour. He was completely at ease.

'As for my love life,' he went on, flicking his cigarette, 'I don't know. When I go out with a girl . . . '

Half a dozen soldiers came down the corridor. One of them, squeezed into his uniform, looked as though he had just left primary school. When they saw their friend, the tubby one gave the tall soldier behind him a couple of obvious nudges. Drawing level, the tall one winked and said, 'Cheers, Tito.'

There were guffaws, low whistling, and a 'Nice work!' Tito turned red and, half flattered, half annoyed, replied with a slight wave. He did not want them butting in.

'As I was saying, the only one I talk to about my love life is my mate. Living with my old man and my grandfather the way I do – and things being what they are today – how could I tell them? My grandfather's from Italy, so you can guess the way he goes on about women – unless they're in black from head to foot and never lift their eyes from the ground. That's why – the way things are today, women wanting to be just like men and all – fine, women ought to do military service too. You're laughing, but why not? Six months – that's not going to kill anyone. It's an experience everyone should have.'

Both the soldier's words and his ideas were like the clothes mothers buy, two sizes too large, for their children to grow into.

'Now me,' Tito went on, 'I'm not a very sociable type. For me it's straight to work and from work straight home, like Perón used to say. Do you work?'

'Yes.' Jorgelina hesitated. 'I'm a teacher.'

'Ah,' said the soldier, and it looked as if that was all he was going to say. Suddenly he blurted out, 'I packed school in when I was twelve. I'd had enough of studying. Now work, that's something else. When I get out of the army, my old job's waiting. It's in a furniture factory in Lomas de Zamora. Summers, when it closes down, I sell ice cream in La Salada.' Here he got excited. 'You know La Salada?'

Jorgelina had no idea where La Salada was but she said yes, she'd once been through it. The boy gaped. He was happy.

'Really? That's where the lads all meet up. We have our good times. Drinking maté' – with the index finger of one hand he pressed back the little finger of the other – 'that's what we mostly do. Then there's smoking. Ah, and one other one – I almost forgot – birds.'

'Birds?' Jorgelina felt drowsy from the swaying of the train. 'Do they breed birds in La Salada?'

'No, no,' said Tito. 'Last year I got into birds. It's the latest thing. Especially goldfinches. It takes patience. My grandfather taught me. He has a stall at the bird market in Pompeya. He was always going on about Italy and the war. When I was a child, he was always saying, "The fear of the war, hunger of the war, you know what is that?" That's where the songbirds went – into the pot – and my grandfather never lost the habit. Every once in a while he'd sing like a goldfinch or a canary, and my uncle would look all over for it and find it on his plate. But later on, no. Later on, my grandfather got fond of them and now he won't let you near their cage. Me, last year, I almost sold one. If it sings off key, it's no good. I used to go out into the country with the best looking one in a little cage. You have to take it out into the country if you want it to learn to sing. It's the song, the trill. The trill's the thing they want.'

The carriage door opened, and a peremptory voice said, 'Tickets, please!'

Tito fidgeted. 'Here he comes,' he said.

'Don't worry,' said Jorgelina, 'everything will be all right.'

The boy had stood up, as if at the authority of the guard's uniform and outstretched hand.

'This boy was behind me in the queue. He didn't have time to buy a ticket. He had to run for the train.' Jorgelina flashed the guard a smile.

'I'll believe you,' the guard said.

The soldier was overjoyed and gave Jorgelina a conspiratorial grin.

'So you've been to La Salada,' he said, picking up the conversation again. Suddenly he struck his forehead with the flat of his hand. 'By the way, I still don't know your name. Mine's Mario, but I'm called Tito.'

'How do you do, Tito. My name's Jorgelina, don't laugh.'

The boy seemed surprised that Jorgelina could think he might laugh at her name. He laughed – but because he was happy.

'It's an odd name, very pretty though,' he said. 'I like it. Nowadays girls have names like – let's see – Marta, Alicia. They're so . . .' He trailed off, searching for a word like 'common' but unable to come up with anything.

'Pedestrian,' he said suddenly, and he stared off into space, amazed at himself. When he recovered he went on. 'I know quite a few girls in La Salada. I have a dual personality.'

He produced this information without a change of expression.

'What was that?' asked Jorgelina.

'You mean the dual personality?' said the boy, pleased with the effect he had created. 'First, why don't you take down my address in Azul in case . . . who knows, in case some time you feel like writing to me.'

Jorgelina wrote down a complicated address, consisting of divisions and barracks. Tito watched closely to see that she made no mistakes.

'Sure, one side of me likes staying at home – you know, my love life and all. My other side's got the lads in La Salada.' He leaned back and looked at her. He had grown serious. 'You have a boy-friend?'

[52]

Jorgelina felt an instant, enormous affection for the boy's round face and shorn head.

'I haven't got a boy-friend, Tito. I'm married.'

Astonished, the soldier went on looking at her. It crossed Jorgelina's mind that the next question would be, How old are you? The boy was eighteen, she thirty. He was going to feel crushed, perhaps cheated. He might even wonder whether to go on talking to her in the familiar *vos*. She decided that if he asked she'd say straight out, I've got ten years on you – I'm twenty-eight. But for some reason she couldn't put a finger on, this sounded worse.

'The man with the beard who saw you off – was he your husband? I thought he was your dad.'

Jorgelina winced. It was true that Nicolás was fifteen years older than she, but the dad bit was too much. Why hadn't he said father? She supposed that father was outside the boy's range but all the same she felt offended. The word was patronizing. It went with the morning 'Eat your breakfast now' and the nightly 'Don't be home late'. The boy had hit the nail on the head.

'Do you think that's the way I'd say goodbye to my dad?' Jorgelina sounded aggressive and made a point of emphasizing the last word. Despite her rising anger, she managed to see the discrepancy between what she had just said and what had actually happened. Her goodbye to Nicolás had taken only a moment, quite apart from the fact that he hated any sort of demonstrativeness in public. The boy lowered his gaze and examined his hands. He's gone back into his shell, Jorgelina thought. The boy's sadness was real – short-lived but real. There was a poignancy about the way all his feelings were reflected in his face, so that you could not help imagining what the world and people would do to him. He was going to suffer. This was clear from the contrast between his well-developed body and his childish face.

Pulling himself together, he raised his head and said, 'So that was your husband. What's he do? Where does he work?'

It's going to get worse, Jorgelina thought.

'He's a painter,' she said, foreseeing the rest of the conversation. The soldier would ask, House-painter?

'House-painter?' the boy asked. Deep inside, he felt easier.

'No,' Jorgelina said. 'He paints pictures.'

'Ah,' said Tito, and he looked at her in a different way, as
if he'd had an inkling about something all along and had just
had his suspicions confirmed.

Jorgelina thought about Nicolás. His bare feet on the drop
cloth under his easel, his baggy, paint-stained trousers tied up
with what must have been a gaucho's belt. His controlled
tenseness in front of a canvas. And most of all his eyes –
obsessed eyes fixed on that white space. She looked out of the
window. She was not going to talk about pictures. The night
was pitch black. Rivulets ran down the pane, widening as they
went. The silence drew out for another minute. Then Jorgelina
turned from the window and asked, 'What about you – have
you got a girl-friend?'

Tito, who had been pulling the stuffing out of one of the
arm rests, cheered up again.

'Well, I know quite a few girls in La Salada. That's what
I mean about my dual personality. Me myself, you see, I like
being on my own. But yes, I know loads of girls. All a bit silly
– well, not all. There are two I like. I'm really crazy about
one.'

He paused, glancing at Jorgelina out of the corner of his eye.
'Tell you what. Once one of her girl-friends asked, "Do you
fancy Mariela?" I said, "Matter of fact, I do." "Then you'll
have to go to the dance," she said. "If you don't, you've had
it." I went and I asked Mariela to dance. Afterwards I walked
her home. We talked. I fancy her because she thinks like me.'

He seemed to be pondering something. At last he said, 'We
think the same way. Anyway, we used to go out together and
talk and talk. We agreed on things.' The boy stopped, then
went on with conviction. 'Yes, when her girl-friend asked how
we were getting on, I said, "Fine, we're going out together;
we agree on things."' He looked at Jorgelina. 'You and your
husband – do you agree on things?'

'Sometimes,' Jorgelina said.

'Her girl-friend asked me if I'd kissed Mariela, and I said not yet. She said, "Go on, then. What are you waiting for, you've got to kiss her." Next time I went to see her, I kissed her.' The soldier was very pleased with this turn of events. His gloom of a moment ago had vanished. 'Summer ended, and then came the toughest part. I had to speak to her father.'

'Whew,' gasped Jorgelina, his mood infecting her.

But Tito put out a hand as if to say, Hold on, and he laughed with his big childish mouth.

'Hold on,' Tito said. 'Don't worry, I know her father. "Victorio," I said, "I want to see your daughter. Can I come to your house?" "You're only just out of nappies," he said, "and she's still in them. If you want to call in as a friend, come whenever you like. But if you're going to take her out, consider yourself engaged to her, understand?" Victorio's very serious. That's what he said. "Consider yourself engaged." '

Tito looked at Jorgelina. 'I don't know what happened to me, I felt something here.' He pointed to his chest. 'I didn't like what Victorio said; it gave me an odd feeling. For a year I didn't see her again. He's crazy, that Victorio – all that nonsense about nappies.'

'You didn't see her for a year?' Jorgelina exclaimed.

'That's right,' said the soldier. He shrugged and laughed. 'That's how I am in my love life. The next summer I saw her again. She had a boy-friend, but I didn't know about it. One day she asked me for some water to make maté. "So now you don't say hello any more when you're out with your friends?" she said. I said, "Who fed you that gossip?" "It's what they say," she said. "And who's asking me to explain?" I said.'

He looked at Jorgelina. Probably he wanted the conversation to sound sparkling – the way he remembered it. The effort made him frown. His eyes went from Jorgelina to the corridor and back. The words seemed to have exhausted his powers of invention.

'What a laugh,' he went on, cheerful again. 'I grabbed her and said, "How did you get that burn on your arm?" And I

[55]

touched the scab with my finger. "Look out, you're being watched," she said. "Who by?" I asked. "My boy-friend," she said, "here he comes for the water." That's how I found out she had a boy-friend. But this boy-friend's a weed, and I couldn't give a toss for him. I'm passing her house and there they are in the doorway. Not a toss. But if I get him alone, I'll kick the stuffing out of him.'

Tito laughed.

'Once while she was going out with him, she came with my grandfather to see me at Azul. She and I walked hand in hand the whole afternoon alongside the tracks. It was April, I'll always remember that.'

He fell silent for a moment, then he went on.

'One day, I was on my way to La Salada. The bus goes right by her house. She and the boy-friend were at the stop saying goodbye, and she got on alone. We travelled together, and afterwards I carried her bag. That boy-friend of hers is an odd one. I don't care, I'm still going to ask her to come and see the birds. She's the prettiest girl in La Salada.'

As the soldier's story advanced, he fell more and more in love. Then he was silent. The conversation had reached an impasse, and there was nothing Jorgelina could talk about. She felt sad. She would have liked the boy to have gone on talking. His words had traced a small luminous line across the darkness of the journey. She looked at Tito. He seemed completely wrapped up in himself. Suddenly, the lights went out. Jorgelina made up her mind.

'I'm going to the dining-car,' she said. 'I have to read some things. Before we get to Azul, I'll come and say goodbye.'

The boy said nothing. He sat stock-still. As if he's been deserted, thought Jorgelina. Picking up her books and hand-bag, she left.

The dining-car was empty. She sat down and ordered a cup of coffee. Mysteriously, the place was more conducive to thought. After a while she lowered her eyes to the book and began again at chapter three.

The train stopped in Azul. A voice announced that there

would be a wait of ten minutes. Jorgelina gave a start. She had lost track of the time. Hurriedly, she called the waiter and paid. She had to get back to her seat before the boy got out.

Along the now-lighted corridor she bumped into groups of soldiers. As she went on, she bent to look through the windows. She had to get there in time. If she didn't find Tito she would feel bad. At last she reached her compartment. The soldier was nowhere to be seen. This can't be, she thought, he must be somewhere around.

She rushed to her seat and pulled down the window. On the enormous platform soldiers wandered round like sleep-walkers; others milled about in small knots, giving each other friendly slaps on the back and stamping their boots on the ground among the little clouds of steam. All at once, Jorgelina saw him beside the station entrance. He was staring at her. She raised her hand and waved to him as she peered out of the window.

She stood there, not moving, her hand upraised. She would never see his face again. She no sooner thought this when the boy approached. By now there was hardly anyone left on the platform. He's forgotten something, Jorgelina imagined. Since he was travelling without luggage, what could it be? More-over, the soldier was approaching slowly, almost hesitantly. She sat down. With his enormous tanned hand, the boy grasped the window sill.

'Are you going to come to the bird market?' he said without looking at her. 'I'll give you a goldfinch.'

Jorgelina placed her hand over his.

'Some day I'll come.'

'I want to tell you something. I didn't think that man was your dad.'

Only then did he lift his head and look at her. The gloom had spread from his eyes to his mouth.

'And what I said isn't really true either. About Mariela. I don't have a girl-friend.'

'Never mind,' said Jorgelina. 'It's a good story all the same.'

[57]

The boy did not seem to agree. Meekly, he dropped his hand from the window. The engine whistled. Slowly, the train began to move.

'Will you write to me?'

'Yes,' said Jorgelina, 'I'll write to you.'

AN ENGLISHWOMAN
IN MOJÁCAR

Vlady Kociancich

Somewhere in the world, perhaps in a European city (not necessarily London) is an Englishwoman whom I remember and whose fate troubles me. The woman is unaware that she exists through me, leading a vicarious life in Buenos Aires, and – what would distress her still more – that I bore people whom she cannot possibly imagine with the tale of her love life.

The story of the Englishwoman is a love story and a sad one. Sad because two people loved each other and something drove them apart. Sad because for me as well as for the lovers (though in my case, as an involuntary witness, it was inevitable, since I was unfamiliar with that love affair, those people, the Englishwoman herself, whose name I never even learned), it all came down to a conversation overheard from a distance, a misunderstanding, and two or three wrong moves. Otherwise, it might have been a happy story.

I wonder if, without the Englishwoman and her lover, Mojácar would have any reality in my memory other than that of an Almería beach, less Spanish than Moorish, a modern hotel poised as if about to take flight into its own day and age of motorways and electronic gadgetry on a Mediterranean coast that still hints of Phoenician ships breasting the horizon in search of African palms, and the heights of the Sierra de Baza blinding under the sun.

But the real Mojácar is much higher up, at the top of a mountain, a tiny Moorish village overhanging another sort of sea – the harsh undulations of the desert, where the glare is so bright it hurts the eye and evenings turns a fierce, hallucinatory red. Thirty years ago, it's said, the women of Mojácar still wore the veil. The small courtyards, the narrow, stepped alleyways, the white ribbon of walls and pens evoke black eyes in a cut-off face, but the women of today belong to another order of darkness. They are blondes from cold countries, tourists with faces avid – almost desperate – for the sun. And those Spaniards one sees also have an air of exile, of unconscious remorse for inhabiting that land from which they cast out the Moors and which so many centuries later still inflicts on the victors the punishment of desolation, in the way that a woman taken by force resigns herself to possession but will never surrender the sensuality or sweetness for which she was coveted and made captive.

We came – my husband and I – from Granada. Mojácar was going to be a day of rest by the sea after an exhausting car journey through bend after bend, past endless rock with islands of ancient olive groves. The Mediterranean was my great dream, and when after lunch my husband went up to our room for a nap I stayed on the terrace.

The hotel, halfway between Mojácar, which clung like a white flower to the mountainside, and the Mediterranean, a curving bay below, offered up to sea and sky an outsize terrace, with a swimming pool, tables, deck chairs, and brightly-coloured umbrellas, where the last few guests of the season, rather than bunch together, had scattered themselves. I threw myself down on a reclining chair and looked at the two-fold sky, the two-fold blue, with the absolute certainty that I could spend the rest of my life there admiring that landscape. A couple of minutes later, I was yawning with boredom. To amuse myself, I began to study the others.

There was a young couple who played with their little daughter. The man was tall and had a shaggy blond beard; he roared with laughter as he made himself into a bronzed tree for his daughter to climb. The wife reminded me of one of

Bergman's actresses. Swedish, I thought, extending that nationality to the whole family. They made a charming group – three beautiful, innocent beings – radiating a light as pure as that of the mid-afternoon sky, and Bergman's camera could have used them to illuminate the anguished wastelands of his films. When I heard the three speak German, it saddened me. One lives to be corrected.

At that very moment, new people erupted onto the scene. They were those strange Britons who travel as a family and who, having reluctantly left the dog or cat with neighbours, find it so hard to leave London to its streets that they drag it stubbornly with them. Three generations made up an ill-matched group of individuals who all had the possessive and at the same time superior look of people who once had an empire that they visit now as tourists and find in complete decadence.

Bizarrely dressed for the Spanish summer, they went over to the pool and, sizing up their surroundings, heaped on the grass a jumble of bags, bundles, air mattresses, sweaters, and towels. As if they were stranded in the middle of a desert and lying in wait for the savages, they spoke loudly, defiantly, in their cockney voices. Each had picked up a book, and they chatted and read, both at the same time, with the skill of circus jugglers. It amused me to hear that city dialect, which lifted one out of the Almería sun and away to the misty grey and tearful green of London parks.

Compared to the beautiful German family and the British tribe, the other guests seemed lacklustre. A fat woman, who swam in the pool with the cautious movements of an ageing animal; a heavily pregnant Spanish woman, with a pale, nun-like face, and a husband who, transistor radio glued to his ear, was absorbed in a football match; and two youths who had parked their motor cycles beside the bar and were drinking out of tall glasses, in silence, without looking at each other. From where I was, I couldn't see the Englishwoman and her lover; they were at the far end of the pool and the sun was in my eyes. I didn't even see them when, just as I decided to go up to our room and have a nap, the water tempted me and I dived in.

I remember the glare of the sun above and the sky-blue reflection off the tiles at the bottom of the pool. Half blinded by so much light, I closed my eyes and floated on my back in a watery indolence that was rather like sleep. Then I heard a man's voice, a sad, listless voice.

'You know I need a bit of encouragement.'

Clearly preceded by another sentence, which I had missed, the words came to me like an arrow out of the blue. It was rather a soft arrow, whose butt end possibly had a line attached to it that led somewhere, but I did not open my eyes nor did I look towards the voice, perhaps because, although sad, its oddly neutral tone stripped the strange remark of any interest. I simply assumed it was one of the British group I had seen, one who did not speak cockney.

I was still swimming when I heard the Englishwoman. That is, I heard a woman's voice speaking an educated English, so clear and precise, so elegant, that I corrected myself. No, I reflected, these two are not from that family. But I didn't turn round to confirm this, for suddenly the woman's voice rose, harsh and heavy with anguish.

'Please try and understand. I couldn't bear another night like that, more torture. It's too much. I can't cope with it.'

Still constrained by syntax, a cultured accent, and the musical quality of that unseen throat, the voice struggled with itself; it threatened to burst the bounds of words.

'I know what you're going to say. Yes, it's true, I don't deny it. I've never denied it, but in spite of everything . . .'

The woman fell silent. The man said nothing either. In the silence, remembering his opening remark, I felt a pang of shame so sudden and inexplicable – but at the same time so real – that to cool my burning face I sank down and began to swim away from them.

Then, as if the Englishwoman had noticed my flight and, needing a witness, wanted to prevent it, I heard her beg:

'Please, please, don't make me do it. Oh, God, I love you.'

I could tell she was going to cry and for some reason I stopped.

'Don't get hysterical,' the man said.

It was what I would have told her. Not to cry here, on a terrace full of people without a wall, plant, or corner where she could hide her tears, or in this air, which carried the least little sound like a loudspeaker. But the man's prudence made me indignant. After all, he too was a leading player in the story and the cause of half their pain.

'Is that all you can say?' the Englishwoman replied angrily. 'After last night, is that the only thing you can suggest? Is that what you mean by love?'

She was almost shouting. I floated in the middle of the pool with my back to them, unsure which way to go. As if that rising voice were mine, I cast an uneasy glance at the other guests.

Like figures on a tapestry, the putative Swedish couple laughed and played with their child, the British group talked and read, the bikers got ready to leave, the Spanish woman stroked her stomach thoughtfully, her husband listened to his radio, while an English voice trembling with panic embroidered a violent stripe of colour on the white-and-gold canvas backing of that luxury resort.

Close by, on the edge of the pool, the fat woman sunbathed. If I had heard that menacing crescendo, so must she. I looked at her. She smiled at me, politely and absently. Then she turned her head to look at the strap of her bathing suit. I saw her readjust the strap and frown when she discovered a mark on her flesh. I copied her discreet example and swam a stroke in the opposite direction from the voices.

'Don't leave me,' the Englishwoman said. 'I'm so lonely.'

She spoke without hysteria, in a tone of heart-rending sorrow, of weary resignation. There was also fear in her voice, as if the certainty of her loneliness alarmed her. I felt an urge to run to her and say, No, you're not really alone, I'm here and I understand. There's always someone to listen, someone to sympathize.

I turned and saw them for the first time – the Englishwoman and her lover. They sat side by side on a low wall that encircled the terrace. The woman was young – about twenty-five – and I can only describe her from a few details. My fear of offending if I stared too long didn't allow me to take more in.

She was tall and beautiful in a conventional way, with a figure that seemed too voluptuous for the elegance of her voice. Her feet were tucked under her on the wall, and had her tanned body, with its curly, straw-coloured head of hair, not been drawn up – knees against her chest, arms making a nest to hide her face in – it would have been a happy body. The man's hand rested lightly on the blonde head.

He was much older than she, fifteen years or more, and unusually handsome. I had imagined him quite different – a grey receptacle for that grey voice. Instead, he had one of those very beautiful male faces to whose perfect lines age only adds lustre and vigour. The elegance of my Englishwoman's language passed, in him, into his body and into a face where grey eyes, bright with tears, lit up the magnificent features of a territory still young but superbly matured.

The instinct of a woman who sees another woman suffering had turned him into my enemy. It confused me that that defenceless voice should come from a face tragically changed by pain. Yes, the Englishwoman had said I love you, but the man – in his silence, his indecisive hand on his lover's blonde hair – was suffering from the same love. I knew that he too, in spite of his control, which had annoyed me so much, did not know what on earth to do.

There we were, the three of us, for an eternity. They didn't move. The woman wept, withdrawn into herself, the man stroked her hair, and I watched from the water, strangely caught up in the pair of them. They didn't see me. I don't think they even noticed my presence. At some point, I must have seen the absurdity of the situation, because I turned my back on them, climbed out of the pool, wrapped a towel around me, and went up to our room. My husband was asleep. Inconsiderately, I woke him.

[64]

Probably the combination of his drowsiness and the feeble-
ness of my story made him dismiss it.

'So why are you sad?'

I asked him to look out of the window at the tearful
Englishwoman and her lover trying hopelessly to console her.
They weren't there. Without them, the large terrace overlooking the sea, the guests enjoying the pleasures of idleness
– everything – had returned to a simple holiday scene. And
meanwhile I had my own life and my life at that moment was
happy.

I swear that I enjoyed every minute of that afternoon. We
walked on the beach, we looked round the port, we drank beer
in a sailor's cantina, we swam in the Mediterranean, and I did
not once think about the other two. When the sun went down,
we drove to Mojácar on a road so steep I dared not look
behind. Even the car seemed to have difficulty hauling itself
up to the many turrets of that white tower. At one point,
frightened by the sheer rise, I shut my eyes. When I opened
them, my husband was parking the car in a little square carved
out over the chasm.

I have never seen a sky like it – an angry red that turned
the semi-circle of mountains into an apparent eruption of
softly, noiselessly, exploding volcanoes. Behind the lookout
point was a narrow cobbled alley running between white walls
and green doors. The shop windows, like kaleidoscopes,
capriciously reflected the sun. Opposite each other were two
cafés, with pavement tables. We chose one and sat down with
a sigh of content and wonder at being in that village street
which stretched away into a void.

It was the hour of day when Mojácar's tourists shared with
the locals the sociable, boisterous ritual of outdoor cafés. At
the next table the Germans with the little girl were chatting
with other Germans. The British delegation had pitched camp
in the café across the way, and with their amused, scornful
expressions were surveying the passers-by. One after another,
all the guests from the hotel turned up. Then, almost last, the
Englishwoman appeared.

[65]

When I pointed her out to my husband, he roared with laughter. Mockingly, he patted my cheek.

'There's your unhappy Englishwoman.'

She arrived on the back of a motor cycle behind one of the young men I had seen earlier on in the hotel bar. Looking very cool, very happy, with her thin white Indian dress and curly hair, she smiled broadly when her companion put an arm round her waist. She put an arm around his, and they walked into the other café. Her happiness (which had a triviality, a coarseness, to it) disappointed me.

'Isn't it odd,' I sighed, 'how we're prepared to wish misery on somebody else just to prove we're right?'

My husband made an ironic remark about women in general and women writers in particular, and he asked me to let the matter drop. We had to make up our minds where to dine that night – in the hotel, in a restaurant on the beach, or by the harbour – and that's what we were doing when I saw the lover.

He came over the brow of the hill, head down, pensive, and he did not see the Englishwoman until he was almost on her. For a fraction of a second, his face lit up. He lifted a hand to catch her eye, took one more step, and stopped dead when he saw the youth with her. I held my breath. My husband was talking, but I didn't hear. I was looking at the man, frozen as he went to her, stricken, bewildered.

At that, the Englishwoman took the boy's head in her hands, drew it towards her, and kissed him for a long time on the mouth.

I felt the blow the man received and I turned away. I didn't want to see any more. Then I heard footsteps receding, the dismal crunch of gravel underfoot, and the Englishwoman's peal of laughter, followed by the boy's nervous titter. It's all over, I said to myself. It's over, thank goodness.

Night had fallen when, after a stroll through that white Moorish labyrinth, I decided to buy a book. We found a bookshop – that is, a souvenir shop that sold books and magazines – in the same road. A woman, another blonde foreigner, was hanging necklaces made of little shells on nails on the door. Her hands full, she gestured towards the counter, where lay a heap of miscellaneous reading matter in two or three languages. A man with his back to me was leafing through a book. Before I could get away, he turned and, smiling pleasantly, moved aside to make room for me. His smile was so sad that I hated the Englishwoman for losing him. I think he detected something odd in my glance, because he kept his eyes on me a moment longer than necessary, questioning me perhaps and no longer smiling. I lowered my head, blushing.

'What about your book?' asked my husband, who was waiting for me out in the street.

I showed him a shell necklace. I had been too embarrassed to leave without buying something.

'They were on offer. A hundred pesetas,' I said stupidly.

I put on the necklace that night when I dressed to dine in the hotel restaurant. The man was already at a table. Alone. The waiter brought cutlery for two and the Englishwoman's lover waved one set away with the same melancholy smile I'd seen in the bookshop. At this point, my husband began to get annoyed – perhaps he felt a tinge of jealousy – so I tried to put the Englishwoman and her lover out of my mind. (He was now the one I was thinking of and secretly siding with.) And I forgot them.

After dinner, we drove to a small bar on the beach. It was no more than a round wooden counter with a thatched roof in the shape of an umbrella; it was so close to the sea that from time to time a fisherman would put down his drink, slip off among the rocks, and check the hooks on his line.

I shall never forget that black arc of sky with all the stars and all the lights of Mojácar, a yellow, winking fistful of them in the mountains, the sound of the surf, and, along the shore – between the distant lights of the hotel at one end and the harbour at the other – only the night, the smell of the sea, and a few people talking in low voices. I was humbly grateful for the moment, grateful to be able to share it with the man at my side. Grateful that we loved each other.

'What's the matter?' asked my husband.

'I'm a bit cold.'

It was not so. The roar of a motor cycle had made me shiver. There they were, the Englishwoman and her new friend.

I tried to ignore them. What did the mess other people made of their lives, their failed love affairs, matter to me? The Englishwoman laughed a silly laugh. She drank one gin and tonic after another, ordering them impatiently, bad tempered, in that fine accent that now pained me because I thought of the man in the hotel.

We decided to leave; with unfortunate timing, they did too. As we walked to the car, I heard them arguing. I heard the Englishwoman's voice, slurred from all those gin and tonics but still educated and firm, telling the boy to leave her alone. The young man protested. It was late, he said, it was dangerous. He tried to put his arm round her, but she shoved him off.

My husband had started the engine. Standing by the car, I hesitated. The young man implored the Englishwoman, and, with the same anguished voice of earlier that day by the hotel pool, she shouted at him to leave her alone. The boy climbed onto his motor cycle, started it, and disappeared up the hill. My husband stuck his head out of the car window.

'Well?'

I pointed at the Englishwoman. She was heading for the sea, teetering on the rocks. I was afraid. I think that's when my husband too became alarmed, because he turned off the engine and let go of the steering wheel. We saw her sit down facing the sea, hugging her knees and hiding her head, her shoulders shaking.

'She's all right,' my husband said. 'She just wants to be alone.'

We drove back to the hotel. I couldn't sleep. I went out onto the balcony to smoke a cigarette.

The night, which had seemed so black to me on the beach,

was very bright, as if the sea, not the stars, were illuminating it. I leaned on the railing and ran my eyes along the shore, nervous, uneasy. The sand had a silvery edge. Down there among the rocks, alone and crying, was the Englishwoman.

Footsteps on the gravel startled me. Someone was coming along one of the garden paths. It was easy to recognize that sleepless man, the inconsolable lover, wandering around to tire himself out.

I must do something, I thought. Tell him that she was on the beach, as desolate as he, that no one was with her, that she was suffering, alone and perhaps in danger. I must clear up their misunderstanding.

I don't know whether I would have found the words. I only know that, driven on by someone else's anguish, I leaned out to speak and clumsily knocked over a chair. It fell with a thud of canvas and wood. The man raised his head and, before I could open my mouth, smiled at me.

But the smile was not sad. It was an admiring smile, one of complicity and seduction. The smile of a man strolling home relaxed and happy who is gratified to find a woman flirting with him. His smile expressed pleased acknowledgement of a game of glances which had begun that morning on the hotel terrace. The smile was all of a piece with the movement of the man's hand, which he lifted to his lips in a playful kiss blown towards my astonished face, towards my silent mouth.

Early the next morning, when we left Mojácar, I asked my husband to stop the car on the beach and I got out. The day was brighter than the one before, and in that Almería light, which enclosed the world under a clear glass bell, it was impossible to conceive of a single shadow, a single night, a single storm, or even a weeping Englishwoman. There was no one on the beach. I took off my shell necklace and dropped it into a foamy crevice among the rocks.

I don't think one should ever leave without saying goodbye – not so much out of politeness as out of prudence.

COLONEL FAZZOLETTO'S BARBECUE

Mario Paoletti

This is the worst time of day. Exercise period and shower over, trusties back with our canteen supplies, all that remains is a silent meal. After that, another day ends ('One day less,' crows Borges from Number 14; 'One day more,' Lunadei corrects him from Number 16), then comes night – a dear friend to those who sleep soundly, a hellish torment to those who do not.

If I stand on tiptoe by the cell door, I can see the top of a tree through my high window. To me this tree is both clock and calendar. Now, a sad winter creature, it looks more like a set of bronchial tubes. But in summer it brings us lots of birds, our one touch of green, and the priceless treasure of the wind making music in its leaves. While winter lasts, the poor thing cannot help being as down-at-heel as the rest of us. Winter is the prison of trees.

This is the worst time of day. All we need now is two or three notes from the Uruguayan's paper flute and our spirits will sink to our boots. Not good, because the secret of survival in this sub-world is not to disturb the sleeping dog of the mind's balance; when it is at snapping point you must draw back and let things settle down.

Here is where I take my grandmother's latest letter out of the envelope again.

An inmate does not read letters; he dives into them like someone plunging into a pool. Each word is measured and remeasured, each sentence weighed and reweighed. An inmate analyzes the shapes of the characters, comparing the A's in the first lines with the A's in the last, and all the A's in this letter with those in the previous one, and each letter with the ones before and to come. A word crossed out or erased at once turns him into a Sherlock Holmes (a pitiful Holmes with neither magnifying glass nor box of fingerprint powder), and he looks and looks again, examining and scrutinizing until he is able to reconstruct what lay behind the slip made by his innocent correspondent, who cannot have imagined that he or she would be pored over by a madman. And what pain when the letter ends before all the available space has been used and the hurry to finish is disguised by suddenly outsize handwriting ('With all my love and heaps of kisses'). If you really loved me, you heartless bitch, you would not waste those four magnificent lines of juicy white paper that make the difference between poverty and wealth.

But it is not like that for me, because my illiterate grandmother dictates her letters to her neighbour doña Amelia's grand-daughter, who does the job without soul but in a clear, tiny hand, which is no mean achievement. This way the two small sheets permitted by prison regulations render a hundred per cent. Besides, what would I gain if my grandmother wrote her own letters? No slip of hers would tell me anything new about someone who is one enormous, continual slip and with whom I can communicate mentally whenever I feel like it – never mind letters – so that I am never really sure whether I am thinking about her or in fact catching her own thought waves.

The letter gave an account of her meeting with Colonel Fazzoletto, for whose wife my grandmother had ironed for years. Colonel Fazzoletto was retired and a bit poorly. He was a colonel in name alone, since his one and only duty had been to distribute office supplies to the regimental commands, a job which had not given him much of a military stamp. To my grandmother, however, this man was the quintessence of the warrior and soldier all rolled into one. Of course, she knew no others. The only thing that mattered to her was that Fazzoletto

[71]

might be able to get me out of the dark hole that I had been put in.

The letter writer faithfully reproduced my grandmother's spoken syntax with the result that by degrees her voice began to rise from the pages, and soon she was talking directly to me. But her despair at the dismal outcome of the meeting had made her hurry over the details, omitting from the scene all description of the characters and choreography. So I decided to enrich the letter by doing a Camus – that is, mentally reconstructing an event, detail by detail – which is the way we Inside snatch a moment's respite from terror.

A Buenos Aires suburb one Saturday morning. In a makeshift thatched shelter, Colonel Fazzoletto gets the propitiatory rites of a barbecue under way. My grandmother is received by Mrs Fazzoletto.

'So it's you, is it, doña Rafaela?'

'Yes,' my grandmother replies drily, knowing that there is no point in wasting breath on saying hello when in this sort of business what matters is the terms on which you say goodbye.

From the shelter, the colonel looks on uneasily. An old woman he does not recognize, dressed in black from head to toe like someone in a Greek film, is not a good omen for a barbecue in progress. It smacks of grievance, trouble, death – in a word, politics.

'Aníbal . . . '

Aníbal Fazzoletto turns round, rigid, a knife in his hand.

'Doña Rafaela is the grandmother of that boy you recommended to *Clarín*. Do you remember?'

Aníbal remembers; now he becomes wary.

'Of course I remember. How's the lad getting on?'

Busy taking stock of Fazzoletto, my grandmother says nothing at the outset. Her stare, the stare of someone who has grown up in the slums, focuses on the enemy's eyes and without straying from them fans across his whole figure. The first impression this inspection gives her will be conclusive and unalterable – regardless of whether the person under scrutiny changes, becomes a monk, or slits the throat of some spastic schoolgirl. It is the Last Judgement – but before death.

The colonel's wife, however, is the most worried of the three. She has a number of reasons for worrying: the discomfort that Aníbal will be caused, the almost certain delay of the barbecue, the awkward moment when the guests turn up, and, finally, the disturbing though quickly rejected image of the remote boy they met one far-off summer afternoon, who was now in an even more remote, far-off place. Mrs Fazzoletto could only picture this as Burt Lancaster's cell in *Birdman of Alcatraz*, birds and all.

'My boy's in Sierra Chica.'

Fazzoletto has just seasoned the meat, and he covers it with a blue-and-white checked tea towel.

'I told him not to get mixed up in politics,' he explains to my grandmother, gesturing with the knife. 'But he doesn't seem to have paid any attention.'

'My boy isn't mixed up in politics. He's a reporter.'

The colonel shakes his head in disapproval.

'Look, señora, there's no point in our arguing. If your grandson's in jail, he must have done something. Anyhow, there's no way I can help.'

From behind another sweep of the fan, my grandmother decides – just this once – to give the colonel a second chance.

'I'm not asking for much. I only want you to talk to someone so that they look into his case again. My grandson hasn't done anything.'

Fazzoletto concentrates on rearranging the fire with the tip of a poker. As he shifts one of the bigger logs, it lets off a shower of sparks that forms a devilish halo behind him.

'I'm sorry about what's happened to the boy, but he should have thought about it beforehand. Also, frankly, maybe you should have another think, because what's going on all over the country is due to the fact that people responsible for bringing up the young are failing in their duty.'

[73]

Poor Fazzoletto has obviously let himself be taken in by grandmother's helpless appearance. Meanwhile, he has begun to grind his teeth with a sound not unlike the log when it burst into sparks.

'I haven't come for advice but for a favour. Are you going to help me or not?'

Now it is Fazzoletto's turn to muster his professional look. But his is the look of an administrative officer who only assesses things that have nothing to do with life and death.

'It's not a question of my wanting or not wanting,' protests Fazzoletto.

'Everything in life is a matter of wanting or not wanting.'

My grandmother has changed her voice and tone. She is no longer a little old woman begging. Fazzoletto takes a string of sausages from a plastic bag and begins to lay them out on the grill.

'You should wet them first. Otherwise, they'll burst.'

Fazzoletto looks up, questioning.

'The sausages, I mean,' says my grandmother, starting to take control.

Fazzoletto looks at the sausages as if they were the first sausages he had ever laid eyes on and after a while he too decides to give this unlikely opponent a second chance.

'Really?'

'Yes. And it's not a good idea to season the meat all at once – only when you turn it over.'

'Why?'

'Because it loses its juice.'

With difficulty, Fazzoletto takes the sausages off the grill. His wife does not wait to be told but goes to fetch a basin of water. The colonel and my grandmother are alone, face to face, ready to launch into the duet of this opera.

'You used to do the ironing for us, didn't you?'

'Yes.'

Fazzoletto tries to pat my grandmother's forearm, but she steps back.

'Believe me, there is absolutely nothing I can do.'

'Can't you at least talk to someone?'

'It would be pointless.'

Concluding that negotiations are over, my grandmother pronounces to herself the sentence against which there is no appeal. *Everlasting damnation on Fazzoletto.*

'All right, I'll be off then.'

'I'll see you out,' says the colonel's wife, approaching with careful steps, the basin of water in her hands. Meanwhile, the smell of barbecued meat has conquered everything else and reigns supreme over the thatched shelter.

Fazzoletto leans the poker against one of the uprights of the grill, wipes his fingers on the blue-and-white tea towel, and holds out his right hand to my grandmother.

'Thanks for your advice, señora. I shall follow it.'

'I can't say the same,' my grandmother retorts. 'Anyway, you've been sold meat from an old cow.'

Fazzoletto looks from my grandmother to the meat, from the meat to my grandmother.

'How can you tell?'

My grandmother picks up a rib and points at the membrane that holds the meat to the bone.

'When it's this blue colour it means the animal was old. Also, the fat is brownish instead of yellow.'

Fazzoletto smiles.

'How does a Spaniard like you know so much about barbecues?'

My grandmother glares at Fazzoletto and, for the first time, looks on him with a touch of scorn.

This reconstruction of mine begins to unravel as my grandmother boards the bus back to Barracas. Even now she does not allow herself the relief of a few tears but keeps them for the secret, private, anonymous moment when she collapses onto her bed. Once there, however, weariness overcomes grief, and she will drop off clutching the pillow like someone drowning.

*　　*　　*

[75]

The colour grey must be consubstantial with prisons, just as water cannot help being wet or gold golden. But that particular prison was an absolute grey, devoid of tone or shade. As with the Museum of Arts and Crafts on the outskirts of Paris, which keeps in an urn the iridium-and-platinum prototype metre, that jail could very well have been chosen to guard in perpetuity the precise, unmistakable colour grey.

Sierra Chica was constructed at the beginning of the century of stone from the inexhaustible quarries that surround it and of leftover materials from the English-built railways. You see 'Made in England' written everywhere – even in my toilet bowl, where it is inscribed in a blue that is gradually turning into the general grey. Instead of ordinary beams they used rails, which protrude into the corridors like a row of gibbets. In spite of this, the corridor is our metaphor for freedom, if no more than the small freedom to leave our cells. But apart from the three weekly exercise periods, the Saturday visiting time (when there is one), and receiving clothes sent by our families, we seldom use this corridor. Of those who have, many never returned. We know that, miraculously, some belong again to the Outside. Others have been swallowed by the Black Hole, and we have never heard anything more about them, good or bad – which can only mean bad. (Here in Sierra Chica we rarely talk about these things, perhaps because silence makes them less likely, but we all know that the ovens are working full time. Although our families there on the Outside may have sworn themselves to silence so as not to drive us mad with terror, the most horrible things still filter through during visits. We've heard that in the women's block live rats have been put up the inmates' vaginas.)

How immeasurably long these winter afternoons are! It sometimes seems as if the day forgets to pass, to move obediently towards night, which is its natural end. Night, however, will once again bring with it the anxiety of the unknown. All the same, Braulio, the Uruguayan, is getting ready to play his flute, which he has made out of rolled-up pages of *Clarín* and the starchy gruel of our food. Like all

Uruguayans, Braulio is sentimental. He plays '*The Condor Passes*', which is the story of another great downfall, even if admittedly my ancestors were neither among the victors nor the vanquished, having arrived in the Argentine much later, when everything had already been divvied up. It's worse for Abregú. Five hundred years ago his forebears had the shit beaten out of them, and now it is happening to him. I doubt whether Abregú is thinking about these historical niceties but will instead be calmly sipping maté and gazing out at the bronchial-tube tree, since Indians know that when you get pissed on it's best to say it's raining.

Tomorrow is visiting day.

When you think about it, getting-up time is not good either. Even the most abject dreams (I am sitting an exam and can't remember a single word; her skin is perfect but I have nothing between my legs) hurl us over the walls, and we are free again. Every dream is a rare jewel, magnificent and unrepeatable. Not to mention the fact that a good dream well chewed over when you wake up can provide hours and hours of top-quality Camus.

Waking up is the problem. A man is free in his dreams but once awake he finds himself imprisoned again. Every day in the grey light of dawn, for three-tenths of a second (*click*) you go through the whole story again (arrest, reclusion, brutality) as if for the first time. For two of those three-tenths of a second you are not sure whether you are Chuang Tzu or the butterfly, whether you are the prisoner who has just awakened from a dream or an ordinary man dreaming that he has woken up in prison.

Today I woke convinced that I am a butterfly dreaming he is Chuang Tzu. An orderly, obedient butterfly devoted to making his bed according to the house rules, which prescribed folds and tucks that are not easy to do. Luckily, I have long since got over the phase of domestic complaints. After all, this is not my prison.

[77]

The greatest sufferers here are the builders. By contrast, those who came to the revolution following a succession of outrages are more fortunate. This is the best place on earth for distilling hatred from all directions. Those who joined the revolution with the aim of building perfect new worlds are ground down by the others, who make up the useless majority. A case in point is Ottolía, who has just come into my cell to mend the window, which needed repairing after the last storm. (If I were another sort of man, this broken window could be a means to freedom.) Ottolía enters the cell with his eyes lowered, followed by the warder, who is here to see that no connivance takes place between the inmate-workman and the inmate-inmate.

It is a month now since we warned Ottolía about the ambiguity of his position and the risks he was running.

'They are using you.'

Ottolía spreads a pinch of tobacco on a cigarette paper and rolls it with the aid of nothing more than three fingers of one hand. There have been times when he has made filters out of shreds of towelling.

'I know that. But if I don't do something I'll go mad.'

Which is why he has gone on working for the prison, mending everything old and broken, driven by his need to keep his magic hands busy, and also, perhaps, because this is his way of doing a Camus, of remembering his village, near Ceres, back in Santa Fe, where the boys learn to use a spanner and pliers before they learn to walk. Ottolía is the colonel in *Bridge Over the River Kwai*. One day that's what I tell him.

'Have you seen the film?'

Of course he had, but all he remembered of it was the shocking part where they lock the colonel up in the sweat box. As I tell him the story, pictures begin to be projected somewhere deep in his blue eyes – the Burmese jungle; the British army ragged but unscathed; the cynical American (William Holden); the British colonel, worthy and stubborn; the Japanese colonel, stubborn and worthy (and brutal, like a Hollywood Jap).

[78]

'Yes,' says Ottolía. 'And the British colonel, who is Alec Guinness, persuades his men to build the bridge. And they put up a marvellous bridge.'

Ottolía recalls the bridge's framework, made of tree trunks, and his eyes light up in admiration.

'Sure,' I say (and I am ashamed about being right, because it is paltry beside the strength of Ottolía's feelings for his marvellous log bridge), 'but across that bridge will come supplies which the Japanese will use to kill many Englishmen – Englishmen like the colonel.'

Ottolía has just smoked a Made in Ottolía cigarette. He squashes out the butt on the ground and leans against the wire fence of the exercise yard.

'Do you mean I'm like Alec Guinness?'

I stand there, looking into his northern Mediterranean eyes with my southern Mediterranean eyes.

'You may be right,' he says. 'But if I don't do something I'll go crazy.'

Another day he came to my cell with his toolbox and his warder, but this time he was on an especially unfriendly mission. Laying down his screwdrivers and pliers – English and grey, like everything else in this prison – he began to work on the lock of my door, which was not, it seemed, secure enough.

'Good morning, colonel,' I said to him when the warder went off to cadge a cigarette from one of the other inmates. 'How's that bridge going?'

Ottolía looked hard at me, trying to determine whether I was speaking contemptuously. When he saw that I was only joking, he was reassured.

'As a matter of fact,' Ottolía said, 'last night I remembered that at the end of the film the colonel blows up the bridge himself.'

'Yes, at the end. But right now the fact is that you are building it.'

'Trunk by trunk,' he said, smiling.

It took him half an hour to finish the job. Before he left he tried the lock a few times until he was satisfied that the mechanism was working perfectly. He gestured with a hand to say mission accomplished and put his tools back into his little doctor's bag of tricks with a loud clatter.

'Thanks for the service, colonel.'

He winked at me and left.

I ran into Ottolía again in Spain many years later, long after the Flood had subsided.

We greeted each other with the eagerness of rescued castaways, telling each other all about our respective circumstances – domestic, financial, and political, in that order. Finally, we indulged in memories of our former subworld.

'Remember the time you mended the lock of my cell?'

A shadow of bewilderment passed over Ottolía's eyes.

'Me?'

'Yes, you. Don't you remember your toolbox, Alex Guinness, *Bridge Over the River Kwai*?'

More bewilderment.

'I think you're mixing me up with someone else,' Ottolía replied, lighting a proper cigarette with a proper filter. In his eyes there was not the slightest hint of uncertainty.

Ottolía had managed to blow up his bridge.

HAS ANYONE RUNG?

Héctor Tizón

There are neighbourhoods in this city where the streets are lined with trees, and the single-storey houses – almost all of them with arched entranceways – have inner patios and potted plants and caged canaries. Those who live here are neither rich nor poor, and one has the feeling that the houses always give off a clean smell, of laundry soap and lye, that they are cool yet snug, and that only honest, peace-loving people dwell in them.

Don Juan and his wife Noemí are among these, and, until a couple of years ago, their only child Diego lived with them. He was just over twenty and a qualified social worker.

Señora Noemí, like so many women, has light-brown hair, but hers is beginning to go grey. She wears the same clothes, almost exactly the same, as she did two years ago – a grey skirt, an ivory-coloured blouse, and a cardigan of natural, undyed wool. Her hair is on the short side, and she combs it back without fuss. She can't be more than fifty – maybe even less – but she seems older. In the mornings, when she goes out with her shopping basket, she uses a little lipstick. Except for the two or three times a week she attends church, these are her only outings.

Her husband don Juan, who goes out more often, doesn't venture very far either – only to the little square nearby and occasionally to the corner café. But the two of them never leave home at the same time. One always stays behind listening for a telephone call or a knock at the door.

[81]

Don Juan is retired from the Customs and Excise. For thirty-two years he was, as men used to be, a model employee. All that time he and his wife lived peacefully together, loving each other in their own way. They moved house frequently; that is, whenever the Customs posted don Juan to a new place. Always, naturally, in a frontier province. Here, in this city, he ended up as a chief customs inspector. He never got mixed up in politics, because to him politics was a remote and somewhat alien activity. Or maybe he thought that to go in for politics, speech-making, or Parliament, you had to be a lawyer of some kind. That left him out. Ever since he was young, he had instinctively known his limitations and kept within them. This accounted for his contentment as well as his gentleness.

Nowadays don Juan spent more time at home, and his life was reduced to taking short morning strolls through the neighbourhood where, after years of saving up – and thanks to a mortgage – he had managed to have his house built. He had bought the plot long before. It was small, with no space for a front garden, but large enough to grow a pair of lemon trees at the back. Built from plans approved by the bank, which held the mortgage, the house had only a ground floor. Don Juan would have preferred two storeys, with a small chicken run out behind, but for a low-ranking official like himself this was outside the bank's loan scheme.

Anyway, here was the little dusky-pink-fronted house, which had been needing a coat of paint for some time, in a modest neighbourhood of similar dwellings. It was in this house that Diego had grown up, a healthy but nonetheless pale, nervous boy, whom don Juan had frequently to dose with tonics prescribed by don Cosme, the Mutual's doctor. The father remembered his son now as a warm-hearted, sensitive boy, who burst into tears one day when he saw a man begging with a baby asleep on the ground beside him. Another time the boy had insisted on putting a splint on the paw of a stray cat that seemed to have been maltreated. The

[82]

animal had appeared in the back garden, and Diego had devotedly fed and looked after it, until one day the cat recovered and wandered off. At the time, Noemí had remarked in surprise that the animal preferred dog food. She had once bought dog food by mistake, and the cat devoured it. In those days the boy was in love with Adela – or was her name Clara? – Martínez, the daughter of their next-door neighbour, the blacksmith. Diego and the girl did not go to the same school but they used to meet after class and walk home together. Sometimes Diego went to the blacksmith's, where he'd spend the afternoon even when the girl was not there or didn't come out. He would watch the blacksmith, a taciturn little Spaniard, working at the forge or the anvil. For hours neither Diego nor the blacksmith would speak a word. Some time later the girl fell ill and died from a pulmonary oedema.

Don Juan had retired exactly one year before the night his son failed to come home. That made it almost three years now since he had stopped working, but only on certain days did he head for the bench in the square, where he would exchange bits of news with other pensioners.

Although she attended church frequently, doña Noemí did not always go to confession. Father Raúl, her confessor, had already known her for many years when he came to this parish from a neighbouring town, dogged by a strange allergy which, especially on certain mornings early in summer, puffed up his eyelids, lips, and ears, turning his face into a swollen, bloated wineskin. The gossips, of course, claimed that this was evidence of a taste for drink. Noemí had little if anything to confess, in fact, and what she would tell the priest hardly amounted to sin. Yet she went to confession regularly because it comforted her, and even her rheumatic pains seemed to lessen or disappear when she got up from her knees and moved the few steps to the pew, where she said her brief penance. The last time, her confession had been shorter than usual. Father Raúl was suffering a bad attack of his allergy. Doña Noemí had begun to speak but, choked by a desire to weep and therefore unable to go on, she heard Father Raúl's afflicted voice telling her, 'As God is great, so must His mercy be great.'

That afternoon, dressed in their best, don Juan and his wife had once more gone to see the police official whom the government had put in to deal with matters of this nature, and they were very surprised when the official suggested that perhaps their son had run away with some woman. 'Think about it, try to remember,' the policeman said. 'Then come back and see us.' A woman? Maybe he was right, but what woman? Diego hadn't been out with anyone – not as far as don Juan and Noemí knew. But now that they thought it over, they realized – somewhat amazed – that in the two or three years before they last saw him they had known of no woman in his life. This they attributed to Diego's long hours, first at the local Social Services Department and then in his total commitment to the poor wretches living on the edge of the city in those shanty towns known as *villas miserias*. He was searching for something, doña Noemí thought, perhaps something not everyone searched for, and maybe he didn't even know what it was.

Back at home they racked their brains for any woman whom their son might have run away with, but they could come up with no one. It was simply impossible. And why run away? There had been times during Carnival – Diego had been little more than a teenager then – when he'd stumbled home in the small hours maybe after a few too many drinks and would still be asleep at midday, when his mother brought him his breakfast. He seemed even younger at those times, a mere boy, with smudges of lipstick on his face. Diego would be twenty-four now, and he had not married. But someone specific, someone special – they had met no one like that. Then, after having given it much thought, they both remembered Nora, a very thin girl with big black eyes, who seemed ill. Doña Noemí told Diego so one day, and he hadn't liked it and never mentioned or went out with the girl again. Later she married a doctor and went to live in the Chaco and was said to be miserable.

The official told don Juan and his wife not to worry and to be sure to come back if they found out anything. The police and the authorities, after all, were concerned with everyone's safety. Although the man repeated this a number of times, Juan and Noemí had by now begun to think that what he said was only words, and that words were only shadows of deeds.

The day had dawned bright, with a warm, clear autumn sun. Few people were in the square; it was still early, and one or two women were washing down the pavements in front of their houses. All at once the sun seemed to go in. A man don Juan had never seen before came out to walk his dog. Again there was bright sunshine, and it was like a warm respite in a country grown sad and old. Don Juan began to think about the people he knew or had known. Some had died, others had moved away. Then he thought how deeply Argentines yearned to uproot themselves from their homes in order to follow a vagabond destiny. Only a handful of friends were still about. There was don Lucas, for instance, a retired widower and avid reader of newspapers, who only two days ago had told don Juan about the mutilated bodies that had been found in the river. The paper had not said who they were, and he wondered what would be done with them. What happens to mutilated corpses? A mutilated corpse has neither name nor family, friends nor money, nor any significance at all. He did not read the papers like don Lucas. Don Juan never had. He wondered now why he had not acquired the habit. He looked at his watch – the church clock had been damaged by lightning long ago – and found that he still had time. His wife would be going out shopping at about ten. Between them they took turns to be at home. Since Diego disappeared, the house had never been left empty. Even at night they left a light on, a small bulb to illuminate the doorway. He'll show up, don Juan told himself. We both know he will – some night, some evening, or perhaps very early one morning, suitcase in hand, and he'll tell us where he has been. He'll tell us everything, all in a rush, and then he'll take a shower and change his clothes. Afterwards, when the three of us are sitting down together again

[85]

round the kitchen table, he'll tell us once more, this time less hurriedly. For a moment or two, don Juan realized that this might well be only a fantasy but it pleased him to picture his son from time to time. It was almost real, for fantasies have the power to convince.

Nor did doña Noemí have many friends now; in fact, she never had. One or two, who had been close to her, did not live in this city and they seldom wrote to her any longer. But she was always anxious to talk to someone – someone who would tell the truth, no matter how little that was. She never found such a person, however, perhaps because when one is sad or in distress it's more difficult to make friends.

It's cloudy now, a rather gloomy evening. The street lights have just come on and they seem feeble, misted over. This morning too don Juan had gone to sit on that bench in the square, but don Lucas did not join him. Being a widower, he didn't take proper care of himself and was probably ill. Don Lucas was always on his own, watching the children at play. They ran about the square in groups but never made too much noise. As a child, don Juan hadn't played in town squares but had swum in the river. Hearing church bells, he glanced at his watch again. I have more than these children, he thought, watching them run off home now. I've been a child and I've managed to grow old. But will they ever reach old age? A touch of sadness came over him. A man who's grown old has everything, of course; but for each of us something is missing.

When the street lights came on, he set off home. The little bulb shone in the doorway, and doña Noemí sat sewing at the kitchen table.

'Has anyone rung?' he asks.

'No,' she says. 'But they say the lines are all busy at this time of day. Maybe later on.'

'Yes,' he says.

'Would you like something to eat? There's a piece of meat pie in the oven.'

'No.'

'I'm not hungry either,' she says.

SEXTON

Juan José Hernández

You came to ask me to intervene, to use my influence, my friendships. I do not deny that I have the governor's ear or that I am also on first-name terms with the bishop. But I will never intercede for Francisco.

I hate to see women wearing trousers and have forbidden any woman in my employ to do so. Nonetheless, I am bound to admit that with a figure like yours the trousers you wore this afternoon looked magnificent.

I could not resist the temptation to confide to you my most intimate secret. But what exactly provoked your anger here in my office – my refusal to help Francisco or my indiscreet words? I was astounded to see you lose your composure, that slightly affected aloofness you no doubt acquired from the English school where you were educated. Me, Cain? Ah, Fair One, if you only knew how much I prefer your insults to your indifference!

Despite outward appearances, I am a person of burning passions. If I hide them, it is not, as in your case, for reasons of education. Mild manners and politeness are more in keeping with my languid voice and less robust build. I have often admired Francisco's strapping frame and hearty voice. I admit that. But his brain is another matter. A beautiful head with nothing between the ears, as the fox in the fable knew only too well. All in all, considering my few advantages, I have not done so badly. I don't suppose it ever crossed your mind that your least endowed cousin might end up holding the whip hand.

[87]

Nature has the unfortunate habit of favouring the mediocre and humiliating the exceptional. The lift boy, who is an utter imbecile, has the profile of an angel, while a man of His Eminence's calibre, with his bulging eyes and trembling chins, looks like a purple toad. As for Francisco, a veritable Greek god, he chose to lower himself and turn his back on his birthright.

Your accusation of selfishness was unfair. It is thanks to my position that useless members of our family have government posts, that our expropriated estate has been restored to us, that the Club is again what it was before the bomb outrage. How pretty you were the night we re-opened our doors and you danced with the governor! Embodying our province, you offered yourself gratefully to the conqueror as the perfect foil for his glory.

Until now, out of deference to your modesty, I thought it best to keep quiet about details of Francisco's less savoury side. I mean his precocious sensuality. Although he wanted his motives to appear other than what they actually were, by the time he was twenty my brother was already mixing with dubious sorts. I say appear because are not sensual chaos and social turmoil at root one and the same?

Since you and I belong to the same family, you can hardly be unaware of the penury we suffered after Papa's death. Owing to the outrageous demands of our farmhands, the estate began to show losses. At the same time, I was made redundant from my job in the Law Courts. Obedient to Papa's posthumous wish, I decided to complete my law studies. It was Papa who had early noted in me those qualities of shrewdness and ambition essential for making one's mark in that profession.

I lived thereafter like a young hermit, removed from the distractions usual at that age. Sport held no interest for me and, unlike Francisco, the Apollo of the evening strolls round our main square, I did not waste my time parading up and down in front of young women.

The Law Faculty and my work for the Confraternity, of which I was treasurer, filled up my days and nights. I had little occasion to talk to Francisco, who, to the family's dismay, left school and went to work running our farm.

On the weekends, Francisco came home brimming with vitality. He rushed about changing his clothes, slamming doors, and endlessly whistling trashy tunes that so got on my nerves I often had to take refuge out in the street.

You must remember, since you used to have Sunday lunch with us, the absurd ideas Francisco expounded – the very ones that years later made him justify the expropriation. Mama would smile in her kindly way, naively thinking, as I did, that they were shallow ideas, embroidery, rhetoric, a part of his stock-in-trade as a charmer. We were wrong. While my brother hobnobbed with the farm labourers and at the same time was busy romancing you, he ran around with women of the lowest type.

Francisco, who poked fun at me for my austere habits, soon found a way to undermine them. He made me into an ally, a partner in his excesses. He would frequently burst into my room on Saturday nights and, half drunk, regale me with the details of his exploits. Seeing what he was up to, I pretended to listen calmly. But the things he said heated my imagination and made my blood seethe. I began to have dreams which left me in a state of exhaustion, with no heart for my studies.

It may flatter you to know that in these dreams you often played a leading role. Once I dreamed that we were children. We were playing on the terrace at home and in exchange for a ride on my tricycle you let me lift your skirt up to the waist. On another occasion we were in a sleeping car on a night train. You and Francisco had the lower bunk. I, in the upper, heard your moans of pleasure. Francisco invited me to change places with him. I woke in a state, my body wringing wet.

Obsessed with these dreams, I decided to enact them in a way that, to this day, I regret. I asked Francisco to take me to a bawdyhouse run by a lusty woman known as La Araucana.

You must not suppose by my recalling the episode that I object to the existence of such houses of ill fame. Quite the contrary. I think they fulfil the worthy social function of allowing our young men to satisfy their instincts while preserving the integrity of decent, marriageable girls. But Francisco did not visit the place merely to give free rein to his natural appetite. Besides being La Araucana's lover, he treated her with unwonted respect, as if she were a lady.

When he introduced me to La Araucana, Francisco had the bad taste to use my nickname. 'The sacristy,' she joked, 'is at the end of the passage.' I made my way to the room she pointed out, where a heavily made-up woman opened the door to me with a bored look. Afterwards, back at home, kneeling before a picture of the Good Shepherd, I vowed to put sin behind me. It didn't work. The fire which Francisco had kindled in my loins made me backslide.

One day, in a new and surprising role as the Magdalen, La Araucana closed up shop, she too to embrace the cause of the dispossessed. I gave up sinning.

You may rightly say that there's no point in bringing up the horrors of the Peronist period, thank God now long past. Years later, when that scandalous circus came to an end, instead of returning to the fold Francisco was foolish enough to break up with you. For some reason, you did not blame him in any way. Nor did you seem to mind being supplanted by a woman from a lower class, whom he persisted in calling 'my comrade'. A short time ago, this same person had the effrontery to appear on our doorstep asking if we knew about Francisco's disappearance. Mama and I refused her entry, something we could not have done to my brother. As a member of the family, his rights are protected by law.

I wonder whether your sympathy for Francisco is not rather more than a case of old times' sake. Once again you are willing to forgive a renegade who, having previously sided with our enemies, is now trying to subvert law and order throughout the province. The apostle of the bordello has moved on to something far worse.

For a long time we had our suspicions about Francisco's activities. He and his red-bearded accomplice were both under police surveillance. Who else but Francisco had easy enough access to the Club to smuggle in a bomb?

I have refused to intercede for him. It's precisely because we are of the same family that I can have no part in the matter. Are we to permit a weed to invade our own pasture? Are we to open our door to the very wolf who would devour us? Anyway, it is too late to intervene. In recognition of my patriotic services I had the privilege of observing the story's fitting end. Francisco lay in a jail cell, his hands tightly bound behind him, a blindfold over his eyes. They made him get up.

'Very well, carry on,' I managed to say. My voice gave me away. I did not have time to avoid the sudden gob of spit.

'Sexton, you bastard,' he howled as two burly men frog-marched him out and threw him into a lorry.

I trust that you will understand and that, despite the grief my words caused you this afternoon, you will have the good sense to change your attitude. Now that Francisco and his corrupting influence have been rooted out, you shall be the Fair One of my fondest dreams, you, as you were at the Club dance – a beautiful, sensible young woman, born to live her life among the chosen.

I have just ordered an orchid. I send it to you as proof that I bear you no malice. In time you will receive other presents, which will flatter your female vanity and turn your scorn into a pleasant smile. It may surprise you to find out that in my delicate breast dwells an imperious eagle. Need I add that that night at La Araucana's I more than showed that I had no cause to envy Francisco?

On leaving my office in Government House, I have had occasion to admire myself in the mirror that adorns the gilded salon, whose windows open onto the main square. It has to be said that my new tailor could fit out even the office messenger boy to advantage.

DOMESTICITY

Alejandro Manara

After Sunday lunch they all moved into the living-room, where they went on talking over coffee. The moment the guests left, her husband went into the bedroom for his nap. She thought she might have a nap too, but then she changed her mind. She would take advantage of the peace. Eight months pregnant, she had a pile of baby clothes her sister had given her that she wanted to sort out. The afternoon was cold and grey. She threw a few logs on the fire, sat down beside it, and put on a Tom Waits cassette with the volume turned low.

It was to be her first child, and, apart from the early weeks, she had enjoyed every day of her pregnancy. Her placidness amazed her. She couldn't understand why she had not seen before that having a baby might be the answer to all those times when her life had felt empty and pointless. That she could become engrossed like this in a domestic chore also amazed her, since it was so at variance with her view of herself as a modern woman.

The phone rang and, struggling to her feet, she hastened to pick it up before her husband woke.

'Hello,' a voice said.

'Hello, who is it?'

'Jorge.'

'Jorge who?'

'Uriondo.'

'Jorge! It's been ages!'

'How are you? How are things?'

'Fine. Terrific. I'm pregnant.'

'Really? When's it due?'

'In ten days. I'm thrilled. But what a surprise. I can't even remember the last time we spoke.'

'I know. That's exactly why I'm calling. It was eight years ago, and I was a bit abrupt.'

'You always were.'

'Then more than usual. Which is why I've been wanting to clear things up all this time.'

For a moment or two she fell silent. 'What are you talking about?' she said finally. 'Clear up what? We haven't laid eyes on each other for sixteen years!'

'Well, it's rather complicated.'

'So I gather. But Sunday's a good day for doing things one's been putting off. I was just going through a pile of baby clothes myself. Later I won't have time.'

'There something I want to explain but somehow never got round to. You know what I mean, don't you?'

'To tell the truth, I don't.'

'I think we should clarify things.'

'What, for God's sake, are you talking about?'

'Well, as you may remember, I got married.'

'Yes, around the time I came back from New York. So?'

'The reason I've never rung you or seen you all this time is because I had a problem. Three days before the wedding I slept with another woman and somehow my fiancée found out. I told her it was you, and since then she's really had the knives out for you.'

She had to stop herself laughing out loud, but a splutter nonetheless escaped into the receiver.

'What was that?' he said.

'Am I supposed to believe this, Jorge? I'm dumbfounded. Sixteen years, we know little or nothing of each other's lives, and then one Sunday when I'm on the point of giving birth you phone to tell me . . .'

'It's just that I wanted to clarify things.'

[93]

'What things?'

The conversation didn't drag out much longer. It might have, because he was in full spate, but she cut him short. He congratulated her about the baby, she thanked him, and they ended up saying they'd meet some time for coffee. It was the standard way out of such situations.

She returned to her chore. Later that afternoon she remembered the conversation and smiled. She was still sitting there when her husband came in and turned on the light. Night was drawing in. The warmth of the fire had lulled her to sleep.

Eleven days later her son was born. After the fuss of the first week or so, with constant visits from friends and relatives, she got back to her daily routine. A few months went by and spring came.

One afternoon she invited her mother and mother-in-law to tea and made a cake for them from a recipe in a cookery book. When they left she sat down to nurse her baby. A breeze was stirring the curtains.

Suddenly the phone rang, disturbing the child. She reached out for the receiver but as soon as she said hello the line went dead. The baby was now sucking placidly again, and she settled him back comfortably on her lap. Wondering if the breeze was too much for him, she bent down and picked up his blanket. As she did so, she remembered the first time she had seen that blanket. It had been the Sunday of Jorge Uriondo's extraordinary phone call.

She smiled now at the memory, then she smiled again. Who could she have been, the woman that sod slept with three days before his wedding?

FAMILY CHRONICLE

Ana María Shua

Aunt Judith always said that no one had helped her down the stairs with her suitcases. By no one she meant none of her bloody brothers or sisters. That's the way she put it.

Uncle Guinche said he gave her a hand. So did Uncle Silvestre and Josafat.

Aunt Judith said only Josafat, their servant, had. In those days the rich had servants.

Aunt Judith's bloody brothers and sisters were Aunt Clara, Uncle Silvestre, the eldest of the family, and Uncle Guinche, who was the younger brother.

The Book of Memories, in its description of the Old House, records that the staircase in question was long, wide, and made of marble. Its two flights were separated by a door that was always open and that had panes of bevelled glass. The street door, at the bottom, was kept locked. It was of black wrought iron. The second flight was steeper, its steps narrower. It was here, at this dangerous point, that the polished mahogany banisters ended and you had to use the wall, which was also faced in marble. So much for the stairs. They are still the same, but they remember nothing.

Uncle Guinche had done his military service in the artillery and he used to sing a song that began, 'Now roared' – pause – 'the mighty cannonade . . .' Uncle Guinche said as he was in uniform that night and needed a hand free to keep his cap on straight he carried only the brown suitcase, the pigskin one. So Josafat led the way with the black holdall, until Uncle Silvestre pushed past him to open the street door.

It was only logical, Uncle Guinche said. Why would I go in front to unlock the door when Silvestre, the firstborn, had the key?

Aunt Clara said she helped too. She and Aunt Judith had packed the suitcases together, the two of them crying their eyes out, and in the heat of the moment what with the emotion and all, she gave Judith her beautiful lace-trimmed raw silk blouse. Afterwards Aunt Clara regretted it since Aunt Judith never wore the blouse, claiming raw silk made her perspire too much.

Aunt Judith said Aunt Clara was a shithead and how could she prove Judith hadn't worn it when after that they hadn't laid eyes on each other for years. She also said Aunt Clara knew perfectly well that raw silk brought her out in a muck sweat and she only gave her the blouse because there was a stain of apple juice on the front that nothing would take out.

While she was talking, Aunt Clara took a rag dipped in methylated spirits to the cut-glass pendants of the chandelier, the very one which had hung in the dining-room of the Old House. Aunt Clara's hands had brown spots on them which it was no use rubbing with meths because they didn't come off.

When Aunt Judith drank coffee the little cup shook in her hand. When she drank whisky it made her giggly. The cut-glass chandelier, said Aunt Judith, looked all wrong in Aunt Clara's house.

Aunt Clara said Aunt Judith had a chip on her shoulder because of the way her husband dragged her down. Even as a child and later as a girl she'd always been discontented and Aunt Clara didn't know why. In this, Aunt Judith reminded her sister of Eva Perón.

For Aunt Judith, who'd been a militant anti-Peronist, to be compared to Eva Perón was the worst possible insult. Judith and her husband, Uncle Ramón, had transported arms in a Lifebuoy soap crate in the boot of their car for the revolution that overthrew Perón. That must be why, said Aunt Judith (who did not believe in God), Old Cuntface On High – here she would look up at the sky – punished me with a Peronist for a daughter.

Still, Aunt Clara loved her sister Judith and whenever they met Clara's expression softened and her face lit up. Aunt Judith talked like a man, drank whisky, smoked, and did a lot of things other people wouldn't dare, and while this filled Aunt Clara with fear and envy it also put her in a good temper.

Uncle Silvestre said Aunt Clara had a will of iron, as did Aunt Judith, which was why they were forever falling out. He'd say this while sorting through dozens of tiny drawers of coloured gemstones in his flat in the Once neighbourhood, where he had a business as a wholesaler of dressmaking notions. Years later, these notions became costume jewellery.

To Grandfather Gedalia a notion was anything not strictly functional. The stairwell's marble facing was a notion, as were the chandelier pendants. Apart from this, he said little. He was a man who ruled the roost without speaking.

Uncle Silvestre said Grandfather Gedalia was as shrewd as they make them. When he came to after his Seizure and found Aunt Judith at his bedside he said good morning to her as if they'd seen each other only the previous day instead of seventeen years before when, with or without the help of her brothers and sisters, Aunt Judith had got herself down the stairs and run off with Uncle Ramón. Grandfather never brought any of that up.

Aunt Judith did not say grandfather was as shrewd as they make them. She said he was a first-class bastard, a lousy hypocrite who played to the gallery and cared only about what other people said.

Uncle Guinche said Aunt Judith was a foul-mouthed liar. Uncle Guinche had never liked women with dirty mouths.

Aunt Clara said Aunt Judith was a bit over the top but deep down she was a good person.

The Book of Memories gives no information about what anyone was like deep down. Instead, in the pages that mention the Seizure we read that an oxygen tent was rigged up over Grandfather Gedalia's bed and that gas bottles shuttled back and forth, manhandled down the hallway by men who rocked them along on their round bases because they were too heavy to lift or drag. A famous doctor came and prescribed ice packs and hot water bottles, and so it was that Grandfather recovered from his Seizure.

When Aunt Clara finished cleaning the chandelier she started in on the mouldings of the china cabinet – notions Grandfather Gedalia would have called them. Aunt Clara wrapped a yellow duster round her finger and ran the tip along every narrow surface. A dark, semicircular stain in the shape of Aunt Clara's fingernail remained on the cloth as evidence that the cleaning had been necessary. This filled Aunt Clara with satisfaction.

Uncle Guinche said that as well as being a liar Aunt Judith was a troublemaker and was always turning people against each other.

Uncle Silvestre said when Aunt Judith was small she was very good at football. He used to lend her his shorts and she was always put in at centre forward. Uncle Guinche, on the other hand, was hopeless and they made him goalkeeper because when he ran too much it gave him asthma.

Aunt Judith married the love of her life, which was Uncle Ramón. Uncle Ramón was balding and paunchy and told smutty stories. Aunt Judith said they'd met at a birthday party. At first they'd been very formal with each other, saying *usted* instead of *vos,* and it was months before they kissed on the mouth. This interval is documented in letters that Uncle Ramón wrote to Aunt Judith care of her best friend, Norma.

Uncle Silvestre said in their own way they were always very happy. Aunt Clara said they weren't happy because Uncle Ramón suffered from alcoholism, which is a disease. Uncle Guinche said Uncle Ramón was a hopeless drunk, which was not a disease but a vice. Aunt Judith said it just happened that her husband was an expert on the subject of alcohol.

The Book of Memories records that at family gatherings

Uncle Ramón went into his One-armed Violinist routine. To make himself one-armed Uncle Ramón would put his right arm down inside the body of his shirt, then drape his jacket over his shoulders. The effect of his right sleeve hanging empty was quite striking. Tucking an imaginary violin under his chin, he pretended to play it with his left hand using a stick of some sort as a bow. In the middle of the performance the stick would fall and Uncle Ramón would catch it by popping a finger of his hidden hand out of his open fly. It was an extraordinary number and everyone except Uncle Guinche laughed and clapped.

Uncle Guinche said the One-armed Violinist was coarse and in bad taste and whenever Uncle Ramón announced it Uncle Guinche ordered his wife and children out of the room. Aunt Judith said Uncle Guinche was henpecked and did exactly what he was told by his cheap tart of a wife who made out she was so refined.

It was after Grandfather's Seizure that Uncle Ramón, Aunt Judith's husband, began to take part in the family gatherings.

Aunt Clara said she felt a bit sorry for Aunt Judith because of all she'd had to go through to marry a man who then gave her such a wretched life. Aunt Judith said Aunt Clara was speaking out of envy because Aunt Judith had married for love while Aunt Clara had made a marriage of convenience to a man who was not only hundreds of years older but was also impotent and had women on the side.

Uncle Silvestre said Aunt Judith had had carnal relations with Uncle Ramón before they were married and the two of them used him as an alibi so that they could meet out in the Tigre at one of the fun parks.

Uncle Silvestre's business in wholesale notions did well and he was the first of the family to move out of the Old House and buy himself a car.

Aunt Judith said Uncle Silvestre was a pervert because he was always taking different girls, each younger than the one before, to the Tigre fun parks. But she laughed as she spoke showing she meant no harm since Uncle Silvestre was her favourite brother.

Aunt Clara said Aunt Judith took a whole bottle of Seconal (a sedative). Uncle Guinche said Aunt Judith took a whole jar of Folidol (an ant poison). Aunt Judith said she took a whole bottle of Veronal (another sedative). In the Book of Memories are blank pages and others that have been torn out.

Aunt Clara said when a person really wants to kill himself he does it without telling anyone whereas Aunt Judith phoned her friend Norma and told her she'd taken a whole bottle of Seconal. Aunt Clara was jealous because Aunt Judith had rung Norma instead of telling her, her only sister, who lived under the same roof. When Aunt Clara talked about Aunt Judith, Aunt Clara's husband (who was impotent and had women on the side) left the room so as not to listen.

Aunt Judith said when she took the bottle of Veronal (in those days Seconal didn't exist) she didn't mention it to anyone and her brother Silvestre had only found her by chance as she lay dying in her Sunday best, a white two-piece with a short jacket à la Chanel.

Uncle Guinche said Norma, Aunt Judith's friend, phoned Uncle Silvestre and told him his sister had taken a jar of Folidol. While Uncle Silvestre went to help Aunt Judith Uncle Guinche said he phoned for an ambulance. He also said he gave the ambulancemen money so they wouldn't report anything to the police because suicide is against the law. Suicides, Uncle Guinche said, should get the death penalty.

Aunt Judith said having one's stomach pumped is something that shouldn't be wished on anyone and only a person who thinks with his backside would try to do himself in again orally after his stomach had been pumped out.

Aunt Clara said Aunt Judith was lying on her bed in her black petticoat as if asleep and was making a noise like a death rattle. Uncle Guinche said Aunt Judith always had bad taste and dressed in clashing colours. Uncle Silvestre said when he saw Judith on the bed dying he had not noticed what she was wearing.

Aunt Judith said Grandmother always loved Aunt Clara more than her. She said when she was a child her mother hadn't loved her because she was snub-nosed and Grandmother would touch the tip of her nose and say nose, nose, nose to make it grow and that was why it grew so much.

Uncle Guinche said Grandmother was a very affectionate woman and from the day she was born Aunt Judith had had a nose like a soda siphon.

Aunt Clara said grandmother spoiled Uncle Guinche because he had asthma.

Uncle Silvestre said Uncle Guinche couldn't remember the day Aunt Judith was born because he was too small. Uncle Guinche said he remembered it very well because he had made a point of dragging Aunt Judith's little cradle out of his parents' room.

Uncle Silvestre said Aunt Judith had done the right thing when she took her suitcases down the stairs of the Old House to run off with Uncle Ramón as we all have the right to live our own lives.

Uncle Guinche said the reason he had personally helped Aunt Judith carry her pigskin suitcase, which was the heaviest, down those steep stairs was that he'd had it with all the fighting and arguing and was glad Aunt Judith had finally made the break. Uncle Guinche spoke with his head under the bonnet of the car he was repairing, as if he was talking to the engine. Uncle Guinche really did talk to his engines and with gentle fondling he coaxed out of them what nobody else could. They responded with a purr the way a woman does when she warms up for the man who knows how to arouse her.

Aunt Judith said Uncle Guinche had it off with his cars which was why his wife went around with a sour face and God only knew who'd fathered her children.

Aunt Clara said Aunt Judith's husband beat her when he was drunk. Aunt Clara, who was as broad as she was long, still had rolls like baby fat round her wrists and in these rolls she wore silver bracelets.

Aunt Judith said her husband never got drunk because he

knew how to drink which was more than could be said for the rest of her family who were a lot of poofs who got pissed at the first sniff of alcohol. She also said at no time had Uncle Ramón ever, ever, ever raised a hand to her.

Aunt Clara said she got on the telephone to Aunt Judith the minute her sister left. When she said this Aunt Clara was lounging on her bed in her undies but she wanted her family to know that although until then she'd always been cleaning when they turned up, there was no need for them to think cleaning was her main activity. Far from it. Aunt Clara liked her housework to be noticed, which meant one had to be patient and wait for a house to get dirty. Aunt Clara said there was nothing more boring than cleaning what was already clean.

Aunt Judith said Aunt Clara had not phoned her the minute she left. All of them had behaved like the farmyard manure they were, ignoring her for ages and looking the other way whenever they ran into her in the street. She said once she phoned home but the moment her old hag of a mother heard her voice she hung up on her. Aunt Judith said she didn't lay eyes on her mother again until Grandfather had his Seizure.

Uncle Guinche said when Aunt Judith had her first child Grandmother took to visiting her behind Grandfather Gedalia's back and always returned home in tears at the brutal things Aunt Judith said to her, hoping she'd swallow her tongue and choke to death like an epileptic.

Aunt Clara said if the grandparents were to rise from the dead and find one of their children working as a mechanic the way Uncle Guinche did they'd turn round and go straight back to their graves.

Uncle Silvestre said in his view Aunt Judith had been wrong to get converted and marry in church and should have done something else.

Aunt Judith said she couldn't care less where she got married since she didn't believe in any religion anyway and all she wanted was to live with Uncle Ramón who knew how to enjoy good whisky and live life to the full.

The Book of Memories records that Uncle Ramón had a

large stock of dirty stories, which he hauled out after dinner whenever the family got together. Aunt Judith would laugh and laugh at them but it was always a bit forced because living with Uncle Ramón she must have known all his stories by heart.

Uncle Guinche said Uncle Ramón had guzzled away his inheritance which was why he and Aunt Judith ended up in that hovel of a flat of theirs with the peeling paintwork they couldn't afford to redecorate. Uncle Guinche stank of petrol and his hands were always grimy yet he lived in a flat that was done up in a nice creamy colour.

Aunt Judith said one day when they were all eating grandfather drew himself up and said he wasn't going to have at his table any daughter who went around with a gentile. Aunt Judith answered that she had no intention of leaving either the table or her boyfriend. At which point Grandfather Gedalia who'd never touched her even to pat her cheek or give her a kiss (according to Aunt Judith), got up from his chair, grabbed her by the arm, dragged her into the hall, and beat her. Then he threw her down and kicked her until her whole body was black and blue and he said she wasn't his daughter any more.

Aunt Judith went to her room and cried her eyes out and afterwards changed into the little Chanel suit so as to die dressed to the nines, or she got undressed down to her black petticoat, or she stayed dressed in her loud clothes – whichever, she polished off a whole bottle of Veronal or Seconal or Folidol.

Uncle Guinche said Grandfather Gedalia was withdrawn and stern but at heart was the salt of the earth. His bark was worse than his bite. He never struck a living soul let alone Aunt Judith who had a foul mouth and answered back and could have done with a timely slap or two.

Aunt Clara said Grandfather Gedalia had never hit her except the time he slapped her for throwing a brick at Aunt Gloria who died when she was little but from diphtheria not the brick.

[103]

Uncle Silvestre said when Aunt Judith recovered from the stomach pump she decided to run away with Uncle Ramón and all her brothers and sisters helped her.

Aunt Clara said her son the psychologist told her when someone threatens to commit suicide it means he or she is committing a hysterical act and more often than not hysterics have no intention of killing themselves though you can't be sure because sometimes they go too far and actually do themselves in.

Aunt Judith said at that point in time she'd really wanted to die but after the stomach pump she decided never to commit suicide again.

Uncle Guinche said Aunt Judith went out with Uncle Ramón for about two years before marrying him. Uncle Silvestre said they were engaged for three. Aunt Judith said they'd been secretly engaged for four whole years.

Uncle Silvestre said Grandfather Gedalia was a tiger playing dominoes. According to the Book of Memories, he was.

IT CAN'T BE
TOO SOON FOR ME

Enrique Butti

When my friend Julio lost his wife, I used it as an excuse to begin going round to his house again. He was in utter despair.

'I can't live without her,' he kept saying. 'I've lost everything and I can't go on.'

He had to come to terms with it, I told him, waiting for a chance to suggest that we go off on a trip together or perhaps that I move in with him to keep him company.

In the meantime, I had to put up with his weeping and wailing. He tried spiritualism. During seances, he'd throw himself down on his knees and cry out to the devil, offering to make a pact with him if he'd put Julio in contact with his Dorita.

I swallowed a remark that I now wish I'd said there and then. The dead are dead, the living have to make do with the living, and to delve into the unknown could prove dangerous. It's playing with fire.

A day or two later, I found him lighting matches, one after another. 'Hello,' I said. 'What's this? Gone into the tobacco trade, have you?' He made no attempt to reply. Undeterred by this, I sat down and began to study him. After a while, it dawned on me, quite spontaneously, that what Julio was staring at in each tiny flame was his dead wife.

'Dora, my little Dora,' he said wild-eyed, striking match upon match. And Dorita's face would appear, flicker, and go out.

From that day on he shut himself in, wanting nothing more

than to spend his time illuminating his memories. Of course he had a go with candles, tapers, and open fires. The deceased woman, however, seemed bent on making her appearances only in the fifteen seconds it takes an ordinary wooden matchstick to burn.

I girded on my patience, believing time would cure him of his obsession, but even beyond the grave his wife clung to her wiles. Obviously, she'd taken pains to work out a foolproof way of controlling her husband from afar, not to mention of keeping him away from me.

The slyboots had him on tenterhooks, so to speak, since each match revived both his yearning to see her and the cruel pain of her extinction.

Poor Julio, festering alone there in his house with a habit that was plainly unhealthy! The place reeked of the very sulphur of hell, and its walls and ceilings had begun to turn black. As for his hands, they were a single open sore, and, because he allowed himself no time to eat or sleep, his whole body was wasting away. Still worse, he had so rejected human society that he refused even to say a word to me.

Nothing but his dead wife's face appeared in the little flame, except from time to time her raised hand. Whenever this happened, Julito went all soppy, for he knew she was about to blow him a kiss. He cited as proof of this a draught that doused the flame and finished her off, sending her back to the place she should never have left, especially not so as to upset those here below who were suffering.

Soon after, the two of them began to talk, mouthing their words exaggeratedly, as if separated by a pane of sound-proof glass. But it was not easy to carry on a conversation. Every sixteen seconds the match would go out and with each new one they had to start over again from the beginning. Dora seemed to forget to look the same each time she came back. It was as if death had eroded her memory or in her new dwelling-place time were not consecutive. According to Julio, she was reincarnated in every flame. Her hairdo, her make-up showed that from one appearance to the next the erstwhile shy and silly Dora went leaping from century to century, from this world to the other.

I was doing my utmost to keep my temper and not kick my friend or the little mountains of charred and twisted matchsticks that were collecting beside his chair. Each tiny flare, which set the brazier of his madness alight, gave me a very good view of the surrounding poverty. A dead woman coming back to these conditions, I reflected from where I sat, is obviously dissatisfied with the other world.

One day, in a last ditch effort, I convinced him to go out for a breath of fresh air. In point of fact, I think he agreed simply because the corner shop hadn't delivered his daily supply of matches and he was afraid he might run out in the middle of the night.

As we walked he kept striking matches on the sides of the little boxes and cursing the wind. A few consumptive Doras came to him, marked out for an early death. I felt as if I had a retarded child in tow and didn't know whether to feel ashamed or angry when people stopped to stare at us.

We went to the central post office, where I had an important letter to send. While I was busy sticking on stamps, there was a commotion behind my back. In the main lobby some exhibition or other, featuring wicker baskets or little plasticine animals made by schoolchildren or prison inmates, was always on display. That day, a barber was showing his miniature scale models – St Peter's, the Eiffel Tower, our suspension bridge over the Paraná, and so on – made out of matchsticks. Wheeling round, I was confronted by the sight of the whole display of painstaking replicas going up in flames. And there was Julio, darting round the pyre, eagerly seeking out his Dora.

That was the final straw. Our friendship had brought me nothing but trouble, and it was time to call a halt. Elbowing my way through the throng of postal clerks who had run out shouting from behind their counters, I made for the street.

As for my urgent letter, it must have gone up in smoke. On the pavement, something else was uppermost in my mind. Solemnly, I vowed:

If I never see you again, Julito, it can't be too soon for me.

FLEUR-DE-LIS

Alicia Steimberg

A wash is what I'm after. A light wash. I sit on park benches painting light washes. I'm a spinster with bleached hair and a young nephew at a private Catholic school. I'm a virgin. I've had bad luck. One fiancé died of tuberculosis and the only one after that never got on with Papa.

I've been an art teacher for twenty-five years. Here I stand in front of twenty-five girls making sketches from a plaster cast of a fleur-de-lis. Some of the girls I don't like; they're horrid little liars who get other people to do pictures for them, which they then try to palm off on me as their own. Twenty-five sheets of Canson drawing paper, No. 5 weight, lie on their desks, and on mine at the front of the class the cast of the fleur-de-lis. What monstrosities they produce! Gross, wispy, or wilting fleurs-de-lis, sometimes with the shading the wrong way round. There in the last row sits that pretty little girl who does everything perfectly. She's so neat and tidy, the darling! So like me. When my fiancé came to see me he'd grab my hand the moment Mama went into the kitchen to make the tea. He died, and after that no man ever grabbed my hand again. My only other fiancé never got beyond the talking stage.

I'm a virgin in every way; no man's ever kissed me or touched my body. And now that I'm old there's no danger of that any more. Fifty-four? That's no age at all, some say. But they can't pull the wool over my eyes. Who'd want to grope me now? After the plaster casts they move on to painting. Oh

God, all those blobs of colour, those trips back and forth with little jars of water, that mess on their palettes – I can't stand any of it! A water-colour ought to be diaphanous, so that it barely rests on the paper. This, this is a water-colour, a light wash. Like the ones I do in the park. Green wash – a tree. Grey wash – a church. But how can I teach this to clods who aren't happy until they've made everything into a mud pie? Then there's all the tempera they use up. They're quite capable of grinding the handle of the brush down on the paper and smearing on the paint with their fingers.

A light wash, girls, a light wash. What a strange dream I had last night. A woman lay on my bed, about to have a baby.

'I already have children,' she said. 'I'm giving this one away to . . .'

I can't remember who she said she was giving her baby to. That's odd, I thought. Having a child and giving it to someone else. That's all right in theory, but after carrying a baby and feeling it grow inside her, once she's had it won't she find it hard to give up? That's what I was thinking as I watched the woman on my bed, only then I find out it isn't a woman at all but a man, and he's smiling.

'It hasn't been done for a year now,' he says.

For a year newborn Jewish boys haven't been circumcised, cannibals have eaten no human flesh, the Macuba haven't shared out the bounty of the hunt among their in-laws, Rosicrucians haven't kept the vow of silence. For a year men have not bred babies in their wombs. Now the period of abstinence is over. But how would men have given birth? By Caesarean section, I am told. Caesarean! In the dream I talked about my experiences of giving birth, as if I'd had children.

'I had the last one by Caesarean,' I explained.

How strange, the last and not the first.

'A mistake,' I said.

'But were there no after effects?' I was asked.

'After effects? What's the after effect of a Caesarean?'

'It had no after effect,' I replied, to be on the safe side.

As far as I know, I've had no after effect. And now here

was the man with a baby in his womb, and it was going to be removed by Caesarean. Of course, in what other way could a man give birth? Perhaps I shouldn't think about these things in class. True, thoughts can't be seen, but how can I tell what's on my face, what things may show in my eyes that these girls shouldn't see? I'm a teacher. A teacher ought to set an example to her pupils. And I do. No man has ever touched me. Except my hand. But no one has touched my face, my breasts, between my legs. God, the things that cross my mind. Everyone knows that some women marry and others don't, and outside marriage there are things that shouldn't be done. I have a nephew at a Catholic school. Poor darling boy. He's an angel. This year he'll make his first communion.

'Test me on the catechism, Auntie. You'll see I know it back to front.'

So adorable. I'm invited, of course. It's going to be in the school chapel, which is so pretty. His hair'll be brushed flat with hair cream. White shoes, smart suit with the knot on the sleeve, the ivory-bound missal that I'll be giving him. The sweetheart. He's an angel. He's already modest, and won't let me in when he's having a bath. He has an adorable little willy, which he used to let me soap. God, how time flies. I used to soap it and it would stand right up, so tiny. Oh, dear me, no. That doesn't look like a fleur-de-lis, child. It looks like nothing on . . .

When he grows his willy'll grow too and then it won't be so pretty. It'll be hairy. One's seen that – in Papa's medical books, I mean. A photograph of that paralyzed young man being supported under the arms, with his thin legs dangling, his ding-dong in full view, and how big it was too. His face is blacked out. Did they do that before taking the photograph? Or did they take the photograph and black the face out later for the book?

Papa never knew I went through his library; he'd have been furious. I saw faces disfigured by smallpox, women with one breast removed. I've still got everything, thank God. I've never had an operation. Now I'm old. All right then, oldish.

[111]

FLEUR-DE-LIS

These classes bore me to tears. Going up and down the rows looking at mangled, misshapen fleurs-de-lis. How clumsy these girls are. And wicked. No doubt they talk about me behind my back. But what can they possibly say? I'm above reproach.

Rain again. There's so much rain the sky's going to burst. Here we are at the beginning of the school year, only just getting through the fleur-de-lis, and all the rest is still to come – the other plaster casts, water-colour painting, flowers, birds, the human figure. I'm tired. It must be because, what with all these dreams, I'm not sleeping well. How I'd love a dreamless sleep.

At one I'll be off, have a bite of lunch, then I could lie down for a nap. But I no longer even bother. All I do is toss and turn and think about the paralyzed boy with the blacked-out face. For a long time now even the priest's been fed up with my confessing evil thoughts. I don't tell him my dreams, because they're completely ridiculous. Anyway, they're nothing to do with me; I've no control over them. But to lie there unable to sleep and at the same time to have those thoughts – I've had enough of that. I'd much rather go to the park and paint light washes.

First bell. Five minutes more and this class'll be over. Get ready to hand in your work, girls; don't start rubbing out now. Not for a year now. Supposing instead of Buenos Aires I were to go and live in Brazil? I could be an art teacher in a school there. I'd have white girls and black. Black girls, all black. They'd come to school naked, with bangles on their wrists and ankles, and they'd draw little black people – naked too – big black men and women, with fuzzy hair on their heads and their . . .

Oh God. The second bell's about to ring. All of them black except that pretty little one in the last row, who's white, with ivory breasts like the missal I gave my nephew. Black girls have heavy breasts, with nipples like bell-pushes. A black man presses a black woman's bell, touches her nipple, the janitor presses the nipple with his finger, presses the bell-push, oh

[112]

God, the real bell, it's time, hand them in, girls, hand them in, I've a young nephew at a Catholic school, he has a little willy and won't let me see it, his first communion, oh God, the school chapel, the bell, blacks, whites, all naked, paralyzed, plaster casts, and we're only just getting through the fleur-de-lis, oh my God, oh . . .

MOVEMENTS

Daniel Moyano

In about 1940, at Alta Gracia, in the foothills of Córdoba, don Manuel de Falla was at work on his vast oratorio *Atlántida,* the youngster who was to become Che Guevara was a ten- or eleven-year-old schoolboy, and an aunt of mine called Adelina weighed in at over eighteen stone. Barely aware of one another, the three must often have crossed paths. The Spanish composer's almost anorexic figure stood out in such contrast to my aunt's milky mattress of a body that, if now and again they passed in the street, each must have looked on the other as his or her exact opposite. Don Manuel lived virtually inside his own skeleton, while my fat aunt plodded along, flattening and sinking the tiled pavements of that sleepy summer resort, with its square and bandstand, where every Thursday and Sunday during that time out of time the municipal band regaled us with off-key renditions of von Suppé's *Poet and Peasant* overture and any number of Rossini's.

Ernesto, who was not yet Che, came to our house a few times but, as if unable to confront my aunt's girth full on, he never gave her more than a sidelong glance. Which means that some time later in his life she must have crossed his mind, perhaps in one of those flashes of memory that appear like shooting stars and vanish the moment we try to follow them. I like to think that once or twice in the Sierra Madre or in Bolivia some thread of memory brought Che the figure of my aunt, the fat woman of his boyhood, and made him laugh. And when he left Argentina he didn't know it but along with his doctor's bag he took the fat lady of Alta Gracia. Ernesto also knew the Spanish composer – only too well. One day as kids we were stealing peaches from someone's garden when an old man came out and said, 'Take the peaches but don't break my tree.' He was Manuel de Falla.

It's almost impossible, however, that de Falla knew Adelina. He seldom left his house, or she the kitchen she could barely fit into, where she cooked endless stews for her nine children and her husband. My uncle was a tall, handsome man. In the blink of an eye he could convert a cow, whatever its size (his handling of knives, meat hooks, and ferocious saws was nothing short of masterly), into those chunks of lifeless meat that people bought at the butcher's, where they saw it as innocent food and not the product of a hacking to death that my uncle had perpetrated in the early dawn hours with secret planetary violence. For he was a butcher in every sense of the word, but thanks to his job as executioner all of us – Che and Manuel de Falla included – could eat without guilt. So tall and so handsome. A shame that bloody odd appetite of his for whores, said my aunt.

The passage of so much time frees one to re-arrange the order of events. Once removed from the period in which they took place, these events float like an astronaut outside his space capsule. Here, don Manuel and Che and my aunt come into daily contact with each other and have all those encounters that chronology or chance (or time itself, which, so long as it is tied to the present, is meagre, limited) denied them in their day. Using this peculiarity of time's to my advantage, I like to think (whenever the episode comes to mind again – as with my aunt's tenuous link to Ernesto) that during a certain autumn siesta, back in nineteen-forty something, it was exactly three twenty in the afternoon when the woman next door knocked. As we were all asleep (except the duck we were rearing, which was our alarm system and began to gabble), she had to knock several times before my aunt got up and, poking only her head out so that she wouldn't be seen from the street in her petticoat, told the woman to come in.

Now that there are grounds for it, I particularly enjoy the thought that at the very moment our neighbour was dropping in to give my aunt a bit of ugly news, the gaunt old man in the tiny bungalow on the edge of town – having been stuck for some days – was adding a few bars to his Atlantic score. Grand old man I should say now that I know who he was, as weightlessness bears him towards me, slow and dreamlike, and I too float in the substance of time. Suddenly he comes so near that I can see his deeply wrinkled face (more wrinkled than ever now that the poor man belongs to eternity), as, quite indifferently, in what seems a farewell gesture but isn't, his old-fashioned, mothball-reeking clothes brush the margins of the page on which I'm trying to get down in words and sounds those days and events which for him and for all of us were once reality and now are not.

Telling her to come in, my aunt immediately saw from our neighbour's face that the news she bore was tinged with scandal. As soon as a chair was brought for her the woman sat down, and, seeing ranged round her the nine children, whose heights descended like stairs – as well as the dog and cat, not to mention that duck, smeared as ever with hen-house droppings and looking so silly out of water – she said no, such a delicate subject couldn't be discussed this way.

But speak she did, and in front of everyone, and to this day my ears still ring with the shriek my aunt let out when the woman said, 'I'm sorry to have to tell you, but your husband's at Miss Glass Eye's.'

Miss Glass Eye was a woman of easy virtue, although not exactly a slut. Did her path ever cross the revolutionary or the musician's in those days? Unlikely, but it certainly crossed my aunt's. The lady in question wasn't called Glass Eye because she had a glass eye but because her eyes were so beautiful, so expressive, that they were like crystal itself or cathedral windows or even the brilliance of sunrise on the rivers that flow from the Andes down to the Atlantic, to the Antarctic, to the sea, to the music of Manuel de Falla. And, according

[116]

to her lovers, one of her eyes was more beautiful than the other.

Anyway, my uncle was in love with her, and every Sunday at half past two in that time which is now eternity, she waited for him to come to their assignation. He loved her for her eyes, she him for his six-foot frame, his strength, his skill in slinging cows high in the air from hook to hook while they were still half alive and their reflections glinted off his innumerable knives, until, having duly disappeared as cows, they reappeared on counter slabs as shapes and forms ready for wrapping and carrying away in innocent guises that masked the cruelty of life. He also loved her for that difference in the beauty of her two eyes, a sort of bridge across which she enticed him Sunday after Sunday. With the same intensity of feeling as his – but in its opposite form, tenderness – she offset the violence that he put into his daily carving up of animals.

Naturally, my aunt Adelina understood none of these finer details, which was why when the woman next door informed her that my uncle was paying Miss Glass Eye a visit she shrieked, and it was that shriek that was to break into the composer's concentration just as he was advancing his *Atlántida* by another half dozen crucial bars.

Looking back, I like to think that the notes the maestro was writing coincided with my aunt's cry and that some passage of the *Atlántida* enshrines the fat woman's shriek at her humiliation by Miss Glass Eye. The wail came in through don Manuel's window, he lifted his pen from the staff, listening in bafflement, but by the time he closed the window, my aunt's cry had entered the composer's memory, breached the limits of this small violent world, and become part of the universe in which we all float. Concurrently, the cry found its way into Che's mind as he lay dying in Ñancaaguazú. For time, the great equalizer, everything is one and the same and keeps happening for ever.

While my aunt's shriek lasts (it's in my memory too, lingering there exasperatingly, like someone going through an abandoned house), I'm going to take the opportunity to mention two factors that led to the withering of my uncle's love. One was that when my aunt delivered the laundry she took in, instead of rapping at a customer's door with her hand she thumped with the side of her leg, which was much noisier. The other was that when she left the bathroom she never pulled the chain. 'Please don't do that,' he begged her time and again. But she refused to comply. In the former case, because she needed both hands for carrying the laundry and so found it easier to thump with a leg. In the latter, because her thighs overhung the lavatory bowl and at the same time were wedged inside it in such a way that her getting up had the effect of a plunger, thereby causing the chain to pull itself. This may have been a piece of slander or a joke and was technically incorrect, for all that could have occurred was reverse suction – that is, a flush of water without the chain's being pulled. Of course, out of ignorance, everyone believed the story about the chain. And this, which was obviously fiction, was what drove my uncle straight into Miss Glass Eye's arms and became the origin of the cry that disturbed Manuel de Falla and that at this moment has just fled my memory to become lost among various other demands of time and space.

The moment she stopped screaming, my aunt rushed out of the door brandishing a stick. The neighbour said, 'Don't bother knocking with your leg or your hand, because they won't open. Go in the back way by the chicken coop and catch them in the act. They're having their usual Sunday siesta, and this is the time to punish them. After all the sacrifices you've made for that shameless husband of yours, doña Adelina, you deserve better treatment.'

It was not yet three twenty-five on that autumn afternoon, when a procession of those wronged by Miss Glass Eye marched single file to her house, all nine children in descending order and behind the last one, who had just learned to walk and was doing so with some difficulty, a gap, a sort of expectant pause, which the cat in its aloofness had disdained to fill. The next and final position was amply occupied by our duck, which had never known the charms of sea or river. This creature, in bringing up the rear, gave the whole scene the air of a picture in a children's book – *Peter and the Wolf* or something of the kind. The terrible story of lost love and jealousy, beginning at the head of the row with my aunt's cudgel, descended behind her back in steps according to each child's height, and, reaching the duck's cuddly head and syncopated gait, turned into a fairy tale, into pure music made of the same substance as the *Atlántida* or the von Suppé, which, on every Thursday afternoon of our golden childhood, bandmaster Ocampo played off key in the town square.

I must stress how important, how impressive, how intoxicating was my aunt's march with nine children and a water-deprived duck in her wake. There she was at the front, in her petticoat, hair on end in the mild breeze that comes down the mountains, raising dust from the unpaved streets and ruffling the children's hair.

There they were trailing behind up the middle of the road between the rows of shacks whose corrugated-tin roofs sing when it rains, the whole procession pierced by the neighbours' glinting eyes, which peep out at the scene of love and jealousy unfolding before them in pure reality there among mountain streams of tepid waters and little cold fish in the south of South America, while elsewhere the first atom bomb was about to fall at any moment. I have to give my aunt a place here so that in this three-part memoir, two of whose subjects are illustrious, she will not feel without significance. Time has tried to connect her with them despite the fact that my aunt never wrote a note of music or went off to bring down a dictator in Cuba. But if that's what time wants, there must be a reason.

Once at Miss Glass Eye's, the procession burst in with a blow of the cudgel, making such a din that in sheer fright the duck leapt higher than the tallest child's head. As this barnyard fowl flapped its wings at my aunt's eye level, it spotted Miss Glass Eye kissing my uncle and unfastening his top shirt button. The duck quacked and quacked in its one-note

[119]

language for God knows how long and, like some fire-fighting helicopter, beat its wings but descended not an inch. It scolded my uncle, gabbling away madly, as stupid a creature as anyone had ever seen.

Freeing himself from Miss Glass Eye's arms, my uncle strode towards his wife and was on his knees begging her forgiveness when down came the stick, smack on his skull, and he fell unconscious in a flurry of feathers. The half-naked woman, also in a petticoat but sans bra, fixed the more beautiful of her eyes on my aunt. Immune to such ocular beauty, however, with one scoop of her brawny left arm she lifted Glass Eye clean off her feet and bore her up the main street to the police station with the train of children and slightly less hysterical white duck in her wake. At the station, they all shouted and gesticulated at once, their arm movements making strange patterns in the air, until the scene vanishes. Today everyone but the children are ghosts lost in time.

Whether my aunt ever met either of her two illustrious contemporaries in the streets of Alta Gracia I don't know. Now that the three have become acquainted in this memoir, should the past ever come round again and they meet once more in the 1940s, which may go on recurring through eternity, they'll no longer be strangers but will take note of each other. 'Ah, yes, that face rings a bell,' they will say with good reason.

And if time doesn't come round again and they never meet in that planetary accident called Alta Gracia (for in life, as in stories, perhaps things happen only once) should they meet in their condition as ghosts lost in time somehow they'll still know each other and will understand at a glance that they are together in one memoir. Yes, our lives crossed at some point, they may very well think. That point may be where four paths came together – those of the two illustrious men, my aunt's, and that of the writer setting all this down as a secret witness, a spy who once watched them so that he could mix their lives together, in words, in this other unrepeatable place in time, this planetary accident called Madrid.

I have said 'they may very well think', not 'they may very well say', because when living beings become ghosts they lose for ever the power of speech (a key part of what we call life) and can never communicate with anyone again, except perhaps themselves. Because death is only an endless, lonely exercise, or an eternal soliloquy. In either case, ugly as it may seem, this is different from the void. Nothingness belongs to the gods, where perhaps they themselves are the void against which they struggle. Death, on the other hand, belongs to us, the living of this world, to us and to our fellow creatures, which is why death will always contain something, because life is the opposite of nothingness, and we, in spite of death, are always someone or something in time, which is our path and our house in that vast territory which the wise are given to calling eternity.

But enough of movements. Let us leave my fat aunt and her two famous travelling companions in peace, let no more pointless meanderings disturb their no doubt secret, exciting meetings.

SEXING DEATH

Marcial Souto

'Why is it that death, in Spanish, is *la muerte*?' said A, looking at the illustration.

B drew closer. '*La muerte*? Why not? What else could it be?'

'I'm talking about the article – the *la* – as if death were a woman,' A persisted. 'In pictures, I always see it as a man. Look at those bones. That's the skeleton of a man. And that cloak – even the cloak has something masculine about it. Not to mention the scythe. Would a woman grip a scythe like that? The skeleton is strong. You can almost see its muscles.'

'We do think of death as strong,' said B. 'So strong that no one's ever managed to conquer it.'

'That settles it. It's a man. From now on, it will have to be *el muerte*.'

'Fine.' B looked up. 'You may be right. But does it matter?'

'It certainly does,' said A. 'Male death is not the same as female death. To go back to a mother – for a mother to call you to her bosom – wouldn't be the same as putting up with the visit of an authoritarian father, who would dispatch you on an adventure beyond the grave simply to show his hold over you.'

'Yes, but doesn't it depend on the individual case? We don't all have the same preferences. Some of us would rather be taken by a mother, others by a father. Why not?'

'Yes,' A said. 'The ideal thing would be to have a choice – to be able to opt for a male or a female death.'

'You mean for some to die as men and others as women?'

[122]

said B. 'That happens – and not just because when we die we are either a man or a woman. I'm talking about our behaviour at that final moment.'

'Joking apart, maybe male and female deaths do exist. *La muerte* and *el muerte*. If sex exists before life in order to engender life, why can't sex exist before death in order to engender death?

'But to engender death with whom?' said B, his interest aroused. 'With the living? What would that be like? Would *el muerte* consort with women and *la muerte* with men?'

'No, no,' said A, shaking his head, 'nothing like that. Death would consort only with death.'

B pulled up a chair and sat down. 'I don't understand,' he said.

A stared unblinking at the illustration. 'What we are living now isn't real life,' he said.

'That's what I sometimes think,' said B. 'This isn't life.'

Still unblinking, as if he had not heard, A went on. 'Real life begins when we die. Sex exists, in fact, to engender death, to engender beings who are nothing but death, potential death, beings who one day – inexorably – will go on to populate the world of the dead.'

'An overpopulated world if ever there was one,' said B, looking with some concern at A, whose eyes were still glued to the illustration.

'Death is a kind of birth into a higher form of life,' said A, barely moving his lips. 'But for such a birth to be possible, one has to have been engendered and to have lived. We're little more than foetuses, maturing for this other life – that is, for real life, which is death.'

'Foetuses,' said B. 'And how long is the maturing period for this other life? Sixty, seventy, eighty years? What happens if we don't live – I'm sorry, mature – for that length of time? Will we not survive in the world of the dead but go straight to a world of the dead who are even more dead? What happens to those who die in accidents, who die young, who die as children or before they are born? What about those who die

[123]

in wars? What happened to the victims of Hiroshima, who included all of these?'

A stood stock-still. Speaking like a ventriloquist, he said, 'The length of time lived doesn't matter. The secret is to have lived. To have lived here, I mean, if we look on this as a form of life, however imperfect and lacking in maturity it may be. Without having lived, one cannot die. And the world of the dead needs old people, adults, and children – even foetuses – for studying the mysteries of growth and evolution. For any number of reasons, all stages are required. Wars and epidemics are death's main sources for getting together the work force necessary to carry out its enormous plans for expansion. Hiroshima can be explained as a case of extreme necessity. That day many dead were needed all at once. But it's not always like that. Nowadays things have improved. It gets easier all the time. There are more and more people. There is more and more death. The reproductive system is perfect. Some day death will conquer and populate the universe.'

A blinked, slowly shaking his head. He stared at B as if he had just come out of a trance. On his lips appeared the faint trace of a smile, which soon softened his face.

'There is death of both sexes,' he said. 'There is male death and female death. That's why death keeps proliferating and taking up more and more space.'

VIDEO AND
CHINESE TAKEAWAY

Juan Forn

So this is the end of the millenium – half past six and almost dark. You men ogling us in the streets, listen here once and for all. Women of my age haven't much to look forward to. Winter hits us in the face with the future, saying, See, this year's going to do your cheekbones more damage than last, and the twenty-first century has nothing good in store for you. At times like these I miss the warmth of early summer, the soft weather that until only a short while ago made irresistible forty-year-olds of us, with a light step, firm flesh, and plenty of energy for love and adventure. Not that I care particularly about my runny nose and dry, drawn skin. I know what I am, even in this awful 1997, and from the way I'm walking so does everyone else. For what I am right now is a woman obeying her instinct.

When I entered her flat, Daniela was sprawled on the bed, half undressed, talking into her cordless phone. The television was blaring, and scattered round on the quilt were a couple of old *Vogues*, a small round mirror and tweezers, an open diary, cigarettes, ashtray, and lighter. Motioning me to sit on the bed, she pointed at the television and threw me the remote control device. All without breaking off her conversation. I'm a good mother, I'm very patient, and I know times have changed. But there are limits. Like the acrid smell of smoke, her dull tousled hair, the coffee stains on the quilt, and the thousand other details I haven't yet got round to. Before

[125]

sitting down I turned off the telly and furtively tucked her cigarettes into my handbag.

'How did you get in?' she said, hanging up.

'With Javier's keys, which you gave me last week. No "Hi, Mum"?'

'So that's why I couldn't find them anywhere. How are you, Mother, you're right on time. I just love that coat on you. Is it very cold out? I've been in all day and have to be ready in twenty minutes.'

She'd flung the cupboard door open and retreated a step or two. It's a mystery to me how she can think half naked in front of her own mother. But that's just one more of my only daughter's odd ways, and, because of the laws of genetics, I suppose I'm partly to blame. Don't imagine her father was perfect either. But there's no getting away from it – according to quite a few, this girl is the living image of her mother, barring one or two tiny details.

'It's freezing out there,' I said. 'I'm surprised you don't feel it, even in this little paradise of yours.' It was a cheap shot, I must admit, but she knows not to take my outbursts of nagging seriously. As long as we keep up the façade, she doesn't care what I think. In other words, so long as I go on being merely ironic and ignore the urge to tidy up this chaos or throw a dressing-gown round her shoulders or anything like that. I'll say it again – I'm a good mother. All her friends tell her so; she tells me herself – in her own way, of course.

'What time's the kid coming?' I said.

She mumbled something from the depths of a black cashmere sweater recently purloined from me that fits her a whole lot better. Then her little face peeped out of the turtle neck, saying, 'He ought to be here by now. But you know Javier. He may bring Nicolás back tomorrow night. How does this look?'

'Try it with the jeans. Yes, that's better. Much better,' I said. 'May I ask where you're going? Without being nosey – just female curiosity.'

She looked at herself, lost in a daydream for all of four

[126]

seconds, and she gave me a couple of kisses that left my ears ringing. Then she rummaged through the shoes in the cupboard and her hand came out with a green kid ballet slipper and a pointed black leather bootee dangling precariously from her fingers.

'Why ask me,' I said, 'when you always end up wearing those awful boots? Sometimes I wonder how long you're going to keep throwing money away on shoes you haven't the slightest intention of wearing.'

'You mean these?' she said in pretended innocence, tossing the ballet shoe into the back of the cupboard. 'What makes you think I bought them? They're María's. Wicked, aren't they? She left them here the day she bought them. I couldn't lie to her, could I? Is it my fault she can't tell sage green from cement grey? Have them if you like them.'

'Can we be serious for a minute?' I said.

She glided past like a sigh and from the bathroom called out, 'How much time have I got?'

'If you mean the twenty minutes, plenty. If it was a more general question, I'm no psychiatrist but at this rate I don't give you more than three months before your first breakdown.'

I meant it. I was pretty worried. She's my only daughter, after all, and sometimes I panic when I imagine her alone in the world. The first person to explain why the stupidest daughters are always the apple of their parents' eyes will win the Nobel prize for common sense. All I know is that seeing her suffer this way didn't make me happy. I followed her into the bathroom, sat on the lavatory seat, and, looking at her in the mirror, said, 'Five minutes, Daniela, that's all. I don't want to be a nag. You know how I hate nagging. But lately don't you think you're a bit – just a tiny bit – too . . . scatty?'

'Mother, I'm trying to do my hair. And I haven't even begun on my face.'

'I can see that,' I said, watching how with each stroke of the brush she magically made her lustreless hair glow. Then I went too far, I just couldn't help it. 'I suppose I can't tempt

[127]

you with a Chinese takeaway and a couple of videos, and we both stay in with Nicolás and watch films . . .'

She dropped her mascara into a drawer, lowered her head, and said nothing. She was doing something I taught her myself – counting in her head until the storm passed. The difference is that she goes on believing to this day that it's the other party who should give in and not herself. She simply counts, waiting for the other person to start being nice again. God, how dumb this daughter of mine is.

'Outline your lips before you put on the lipstick,' I said, leaving the bathroom. I couldn't help glancing in the mirror as I stood up – a vice all women share. Daniela was smiling secretly to herself, her hand groping among the jumble that littered the drawer.

'Can I borrow your coat?' she called out a moment or two later.

I didn't answer. I'd picked up the copies of *Vogue* and sat down in the minuscule armchair that opened into a bed for Nicolás. I had to talk to Daniela's father. At the age of six a boy should have his own room. Of course, it's Javier who ought to be thinking about these things. But as far as I can make out, Javier already has enough on his plate.

'Heard anything about Malabia? Anyone interested?' I said.

She didn't answer or didn't hear. I don't see how they'll ever sell that place – not in the state it's in. When they separated, Daniela refused to live there alone with the child. She simply looked at me and said, 'There are things you do only when you're in love, Mother.' And you have to admit she was right about that.

The street-door buzzer went. Daniela came into the living-room and halted in front of me. Do I need to tell you how she looked?

'Tell me I look terrific.'

'You look terrific, dear.'

She squatted, twisted her head to look up at me and seemed to be thinking for a moment.

'All right, don't stuff now. Make him a rice soup or

something light, depending on how hungry he is when he gets here. Video, sure, if you want to. Why don't you take out two? I'll be back early, and we can watch the other one together.' The buzzer went again. 'Leave it, don't answer. I'm on my way. Do I really look terrific?'

I nodded.

'I take after my mother, see? You'd have to know her to realize it.'

I laughed too. But no hugs or emotional tears; she was already opening the door and ringing for the lift. She checked the contents of her handbag, heard the third long buzz, muttered, 'Coming, coming,' and said to me, 'My ciggies, Mother. You never change, do you? Where did you hide them? Quickly, please.'

Not two minutes after she left, the hall bell rang and almost at the same time there came a flurry of violent blows on the door. The distance from my chair to the door is minimal but before I could open it I counted eight knocks and three long rings.

'Hello, my little sunshine. How are you?'

'Gran you know what we can do? Get a Chinese takeaway and you teach me to eat with chopsticks. Mummy has some. I know where they are. Let's. Let's.'

This boy's energy is amazing. You'd think he would arrive exhausted and fall asleep in my arms before even giving me a kiss. I wonder what makes him so hyper. For a moment or two I thought of suggesting he practise with the chopsticks on rice soup and Valium. But grand-children are inflexible when bargaining with grandmothers. Nicolás studied me expectantly from his thirty-six-inch height.

'Don't call me Gran.'

'I know how to buy the food. There are no streets to cross. Give me the money and I'll go, okay? Mummy always rings up and says I'm coming and tells them what we want. The number's in the kitchen, come and see. If you go the food'll get cold. I'll run ever so fast.'

[129]

'There's the video shop, too,' I said, almost won over, the receiver already in my hand and Nicolás's eyes on me.

'I'll go to both places. You call and say which film. They know me too.'

'And what if something happens to you?'

Again I'd gone too far. Nicolás gaped at me, dismayed. I sighed.

'I suppose if I went with you it wouldn't be any fun,' I said. And his face lit up. This child is going to cause mayhem among women in the next century, believe me. His smile made me feel an absurd wave of pride in being his grandmother and part of his life. A monster, that's what he is – a little monster.

He showed me the number again, made me dial, and said, 'Chow mein, say chow mein. They'll know.' Then he fetched the list of videos, helped me pick a film for him and me and another one for Daniela, brought my bag already open, and was good enough to let me be the one to fish out the money.

'Please, Nico, be careful. Promise me?'

He said of course and gave the door an earthshaking slam. Twenty minutes later he was back, sweating, breathless, and juggling packages. He wanted to sit down and eat without taking off his jacket. He had forgotten all about the chopsticks. I told him to find them while I tidied up his mother's bedroom. We sat on the bed with our tray and he got up to put on the video. On the bed again, he turned his back to the television and said, 'Okay, how do I hold them?' as he devoured a spring roll.

He followed my directions carefully, taking the chopsticks in his right hand as I had shown him, all the while eating most of his chow mein with his left hand. But he was overjoyed to have learned the trick.

'Now I'm always going to eat with chopsticks,' he said a moment later, his mouth full.

I put the tray on the floor and we nestled down among the pillows.

'Do you know what's going on?' I said, watching the television.

[130]

'He comes from another planet because he has to rescue his people and she's his mother, but actually she still hasn't had him and she doesn't know that the baddy – that's him, Arnold, see? – has come too, but not to rescue her. He has to kill her. And the baddy's a robot, not the goody though, and they both come from a planet that's in the future. It's an old film that Daddy loves.'

'Ah,' I said. The goody was caressing the sleeping girl and seemed to want to kiss her. Nicolás turned his head and looked me over.

'Gran, you can still have boyfriends, can't you?'

'Don't call me Gran.'

'But can you or can't you? Mummy told me not to ask.'

'Yes, I can. And now don't ask me why I haven't got one. Hasn't your mother taught you there's nothing worse than a nosey man?'

'You and Mummy are nosey.'

'Well, women are allowed to be nosey. It suits them.'

I had approximately two minutes of peace. Then, by the way Nicolás was leaning against me, I realized that the conversation was going to go on.

'Mummy thinks she's in love,' he said, and he turned up the volume of the film.

'What did you say? Give me that. Nico. Come here. Nico.'

'I need to pee,' he said tossing me the remote control.

If Daniela was crazy enough to say something like that to her own son, it meant a lot was going on behind my back. *I'm* her best friend – so she's always saying. I'm the only one who listens dispassionately to her stories and doesn't give an opinion until asked. I was the first to know she was going to split up, I was the first to know she was expecting Nicolás. I knew even before Javier. I was the first to know they were getting married. And now this little monster was telling me my own daughter was in love with another man. Who could he be? I wondered who else Daniela had told. Was it someone Nicolás knew? And how had I not noticed anything was going on?

[131]

'When did she tell you? And don't ask me what,' I said when he came out of the bathroom with that angelic face of his.

'She didn't.'

'Nicolás!'

'*She* didn't tell me. I'm tired. Can I sleep here?'

'Yes. You can sleep here. But answer me first. Didn't I teach you to use chopsticks? Look me in the eye.'

'Daddy told me. Don't tell Mummy. Or about the Chinese takeaway.'

'Don't worry, sweetie,' I said, and I ruffled his hair. 'But don't go to sleep like that. At least wait for me to put your pyjamas on.'

'Put them on me when I'm sleeping.'

At which he fell fast asleep in that irritatingly easy way children do. And there I was all on my own digesting that bombshell. Was I to feel happy for Daniela and a bit sad for poor Javier? Should I be furious with him for telling such things to the child, for putting Nicolás between his father and mother? It wasn't like Javier to do that sort of thing. Maybe Nicolás told him about some man coming to see Daniela, and Javier explained that she had the right to fall in love again, or something like that. Children's minds work in very different ways from ours.

I found cigarettes in the drawer of the bedside table. Turning off the video and the lights, I went into the living-room to smoke and have a think. I leafed through one of the magazines and lit a cigarette. My head began to ache. I phoned to find out the time – ten past ten. Early for Daniela could be two in the morning. I went to put Nico's pyjamas on him, tucked him in, and without making a sound put his clothes away in the chest of drawers. I made myself some coffee and took two aspirins. I lit another cigarette, sitting in the armchair with a second cup of coffee. I kept thinking and thinking.

Then my eyes closed, and I saw Daniela come in with her new love, but I couldn't put a face to him. All I managed to picture was some strapping, elegant guy, a banker with a Volvo or BMW and a year-round tan from sailing or golf. But how does one think up a face unlike any other, especially unlike Javier's which in itself is nondescript yet attractive enough once you get used to it. I saw Nicolás with a room of his own, tons of electronic toys that he'd either ignore or break in a twinkling, his own telly, maybe his own computer. And I felt a bit depressed. Was it my fault I'd been dragged into my daughter's crude, opportunist choice of partner and my grandson's resulting future unhappiness? Could Javier have been so poor a prize, such a bad husband? It was Daniela who had taught us to see Javier's good points, the one who had shown us – her father, her friends, me – that the heart's reasons often become clearer with the passage of time. And had she now suddenly turned her back on all that without even giving the poor man a second chance?

The sound of keys in the door woke me. I opened my eyes and saw Daniela taking off my coat. She smiled at me, hung it on the coat rack, and sank into the little armchair opposite me.

'Caught you, didn't I? Smoking your daughter's cigarettes. You ought to be ashamed.'

But she wasn't the Daniela who had gone out three hours earlier. Her voice lacked the electric conviction that gave it its insouciance. She was meek, pensive, worried – not at all herself.

'What about your Romeo?' I said. 'Isn't he coming up? Are you going to keep me on pins and needles?'

She raised her eyebrows.

'He's married,' I said. 'No, don't tell me. If he brings you back so early, he must be married.'

'What are you talking about, Mother?'

'About the guy you're going out with. The one you went out with tonight. Your future second husband. The man who's going to ruin your life with fur coats, one-way conversations about golf or high finance, and summers in Punta del Este. The man you're about to make the same mistake with that I did with your father.'

[133]

Daniela stared at me for a long time, then, lighting a cigarette, she brushed the hair back out of her eyes.

'I was with Javier, Mum.'

'With Javier,' I repeated. 'Ah. So he was the one you were talking to on the phone when I arrived. You were with Javier *just now?*'

She nodded. I tried not to wonder whether Daniela had heard all the nonsense that I'd been babbling a moment before. I lit a cigarette, inhaled deeply, and felt a sort of smile stretching my lips. 'Why didn't you say anything about it, silly?'

'Because it was a surprise.' She gave a little laugh and then turned serious again. 'I was going to but I wanted to talk to him first.'

'So what happened?'

'What happened was I screwed up,' she said, pursing her lips in a rueful expression.

'I need more coffee.'

When I came back into the living-room with the mugs, Daniela said, 'If I keep drinking these heavy-duty amounts of coffee, I'll turn mulatto.' I chose to inhale the steam from my cup and say nothing until I found out what was going on.

'You'd like us to get back together, wouldn't you?' she said.

I shrugged, pathetically guilty. She chuckled again, as if she were letting out the remnants of a belly laugh that she'd kept bottled up, and she stared at me with sparkling eyes.

'Everyone would,' she said. 'It's kind of logical. Sometimes I'd like it too.'

'What's the problem, then? Why did you say you screwed up?'

'I told him I was pregnant.'

I closed my eyes. My heart thumped. Some of my worst fears about my daughter's future seemed to be coming true. Staring at her, I said in the most controlled, casual voice I could muster, 'You're pregnant?'

'That's the least of it, Mother. I wanted to see whether he'd react the way he did when I told him I was going to have Nicolás.'

[134]

'Ah,' I said, as if I'd just heard something perfectly rational. 'And what did he say?'

'He asked me by whom.'

The silence became unnerving. As she finished speaking she began to shake, until all at once she burst out laughing. For a second I'd thought the shaking was a prelude to a flood of tears. Even when she started to laugh I was still waiting for her to shift to crying. But her laugh was as pure and clear as a crystal bell and betrayed not a jot of hysteria. It was a healthy, infectious laugh.

'What a shit. What bloody assholes men are, don't you think? They care more about being cheated on than about any chance of happiness. The fact is they're all a pack of bastards,' she said between laughs. 'Such bastards that they're rather sweet, aren't they?'

I know nothing in this world to match female complicity. They say it's only a cheap myth, the sort of thing progress and the new millenium will put an end to. They say that true female complicity can't exist between mothers and daughters. Let them say what they like, I couldn't care less about such idiotic generalizations. I know what I felt at that moment.

'My dear girl,' I said, 'you've discovered a monumental truth.'

She stood up and we toasted each other with our empty mugs.

'To a world-shattering discovery,' she said.

'To female wisdom,' I added. And again we laughed.

Then I remembered the other film. Together we opened the day-bed. I picked Nicolás up, she put him in the bed, and we covered him with a mother and a grandmother's gossamer kisses. Then we went into the bedroom and made ourselves comfortable on the pillows. As the warning against the pirating of videos came on, I said vaguely, 'But are you actually pregnant or not?'

Daniela stopped playing with the remote control and stared at me in astonishment.

'Not as far as I know,' she said. 'Why? You think I've put on weight?'

WAKING UP ALIVE

Noemí Ulla

TO JUAN JOSÉ HERNÁNDEZ

As it happened, she had gone there to look after him. Late every afternoon he'd been taking to the bottle, and she, out of naivety or laziness, had thought that in this out-of-the-way spot by the sea he'd give in to the surroundings and change his habits.

That day they'd bought cologne in the local chemist's near the hotel. Sniffing it, such a fresh scent, he had remarked on how much good it would do his clean skin after a dip and a shower. At that point, she'd felt like a monster. His remarks, along with his boyish smile, were so tender that she wondered how on earth she could ever have wanted to kill him. An hour later she was to see him lost in the amber liquid, with no thought of her, full of airy fantasies that he would spend his evenings writing.

So here they were together. A few days earlier, in the city, he'd talked of going to the seaside alone. Then he begged her to go with him, and, feeling that she deserved a break after translating hour upon hour, twenty days on the trot, she gave in. She thought the sea might somehow restore him to the healthy outdoor life he'd led in his twenties, when they used to phone each other and make plans to meet at the beach – the only ones in their set interested in the sun, swimming, and barbecue picnics. She wouldn't leave him. She'd stay with him for old times's sake or for reasons of her own, until, against both their wills, something from outside, some external factor, intervened. So she must go on hating him and loving him, wanting him and putting up with him. Were they not just one more couple like all the others in the world who carried on in this way? At the same time, had they not had beautiful moments together, long chats in which poetry entered the night like the waters of a stream – now crystal-clear, now muddy, now stormy, now almost calm – until in his mind the words he spoke became entangled with the floating mass of green-leaved, yellow-blossoming *camalote* on the river, and, now trumpeting, now on tiptoe, his drunken raving entered as well?

She'd seen the plant somewhere else, she could not remember where. Then it came to her. The night before, it had appeared in a dream, presiding over an empty shelf, and she'd noticed how strong it had grown. In the dream it must have been a plant she knew. There were other plants on the terrace, with and without flowers. This one had captivated her. The white fringes down the length of its green leaves gave her the idea of making herself a full-sleeved blouse. The memory of the plant had followed her here onto the beach, but she forgot it, until, coming out of the water, she remembered it again.

She'd been looking towards the hotel, watching for him. Then, tired of waiting, she turned and stared out to sea. She rubbed suntan lotion on her face and body, donned her straw hat, and let the breeze wrap her round in a way that was familiar, luxurious. Her skin felt smooth, soft, oiled. Opposite, she saw the cat family's beach umbrella. The cats was what they both called them, because there were hordes of them and they all looked alike with their tawny cats' eyes. They were potato growers and – this he'd found out from the eldest cat – they had money to burn. Splashing it around at lunch and dinner, they all talked at once in loud voices, roaring with contagious laughter, and the more they laughed the more their eyes narrowed into slits on their feline faces.

He had made friends with this family, and whenever he ran into the eldest of them in the hotel corridor or out on the terrace he'd ask if they were all going to the beach or if they'd managed to get any sleep what with the music from the bar, which the hotel keeper played with fascist fervour until all hours. Afterwards, like a delighted child, he reported back to her how he'd got in with the potato merchant. He also talked to the other families and had a word for everyone. This amazed her, for she, who could never think of anything to say to people, merely watched the world from the sidelines, aloof, detached. At heart, he was still the actor he had been in his youth. He could laugh when the person he was speaking to expected a laugh, he could ask questions when he was expected to show interest, he could respond with all the sympathy and grace his boyish face and lithe body brought to his aid, because he knew he was being looked at.

If he was late now it was because the amber liquid had kept him happy into the small hours, while she had fallen asleep and lost track of what time he'd come in. The bar with the loud music was his current haunt. Soon he would tire of it and begin to look for another place, one as yet uninvaded by crowds. Once he'd told her he preferred quiet spots but as soon as they became known he would look for another, a place without people, until that one too filled up. In this way, he drifted from one bar to the next, forever on the lookout for solitary corners.

As for her, nothing irritated her more than being left on her own. She needed another human body beside her to know who she was. This is getting bad, she thought, as another set of their hotel dining-room companions greeted her effusively. They feel sorry for me, always seeing me alone on the beach. What should she do – walk up and down trying to pick up a man to have a drink with and never go back again? Or make a date for another time and return happier, less angry with him for always being asleep, always abandoning her to sleep?

She picked up her things – her beach bag, sunglasses, the suntan lotion she'd left in her clogs – carefully shook out her bathing towel, stuffed the lot into the bag, and set off. Her bare feet sank into the sand. At once she felt them burning. Bending down, she took out the clogs and put them on. She walked with the same difficulty as before, the clogs protecting the soles of her feet but hampering her normal movement. Yes, she thought, on sand you have to learn to walk differently.

There weren't many available men on the beach at that hour. Of course not. This was a family resort, and most of these men would be staying at the hotel. Just now they'd be having their afternoon nap. So was he. It was good to be at a place right on the shore; nothing could be closer or more comfortable, she thought, remembering that he had found it. In the showers on the back patio she took off the clogs and wet her feet to clean all the sand from them. The smooth brick made her think of the back yard of her small-town childhood.

The owners of the hotel came and went past her with the fuss and bustle that preceded mealtimes. Returning from the beach, holiday-makers immediately smelled the rich aroma of stewing meat. The owner's wife brushed by with a sprig or two of rosemary. It was partridge that night, she said. The woman, a blonde, had narrow, sloping shoulders and broad hips. He fancied her. On their last trip there, one New Year's Eve, she'd found this out. In the midst of all the revelry, he'd told her that the hotel keeper's wife reminded him of his mother.

She climbed the stairs and was suddenly at the door of their old room. On the previous afternoon they'd asked if they could move. 'So long as it's not too much trouble', they had added, and here she was now; she'd thought they were still on that floor. She went down a flight and made her way along the corridor in the semi-darkness until she got to the new door. She slipped quietly in and came face to face with the same old scene: he was fast asleep. Taking off her swimsuit, she put on a thin orange sundress. It looked good against her tanned skin, she noted in the mirror as she slipped a string of beads over her head. She was putting on her sandals, ready to go out, when, in a voice that showed he was in a good mood, he asked what time it was.

In the dining-room she took their usual table by the doorway, facing the sea. Outside, bordering the path along the windows, was a row of small tamarisks. It was hot, despite the light evening breeze. While she waited, she had time to take in the other tables and tell herself she was a coward who hadn't the courage to give up looking after a dead man. At that point he walked in and, with the air of a young man grateful for an audience, glanced about him, a smile and a greeting for everyone. He then helped himself to wine, knocking it back in a single gulp, while she looked on, aghast at the explosive he was pouring into an empty stomach. Just to look at him made her feel sick.

He told her about a dream. Out of a mossy wall spurted a jet of water. She listened to him; it was always liquid. The dream was getting complicated, until, distracted by a greeting from new arrivals at the next table, he lost the thread of his story. He was unable to pick it up again. One dish followed another, tasty as usual, and they were eating them and commenting on the other guests in the room, the clear sky, the graceful silhouette of the tamarisks. The weather was calm; it promised a run of fine days. Over dessert, he said something to the girl waiting on their table, one of the owner's daughters. She went out to the kitchen and returned with a tray, two glasses, and an ice bucket holding a champagne bottle with a white napkin wrapped round its neck.

'You weren't expecting this, kitten,' he said, one of his hands taking and kissing hers while the other turned the champagne in the bucket. He uncorked the bottle – a favourite task of his – and poured it into the two polished glasses that the girl had put on the table.

'To us,' he said, reaching for her glass with his. He got up, gave her the tenderest of kisses, and said to the room at large, 'This is to our five years together.'

A masterly performance, she felt, afloat on a cloud. His announcement went down well, and those at the nearest tables, who had followed them closely, wished the couple many happy returns. They thanked them all for their good wishes, and she stared into his dancing eyes, which at that moment held all the sweetness in the world. As she went to pick up her glass again, she found a tiny parcel wrapped in tissue paper. She opened it eagerly. Inside was a stylish necklace that she had wanted very much. She put it on at once; as she asked him to do up the clasp, she got a waft of some smell she could not identify, a cross between cinnamon and sheepskin. If she mentioned it, he'd say she was crazy, so she kept it to herself and went on sniffing furtively, trying to detect which of the two it was. She was sure that the smell came from neither the kitchen nor the necklace.

Since living alone he had become more generous. Before that, when they were together, he'd spent every penny of his small earnings, and the occasional rise or any little extra income always went on himself – a pair of good shoes, a finer shirt, more expensive trousers, long taxi rides. This was what had made her begin to hate him. More so when her friends pointed out that while she economized on her clothes, he dressed as if he came from another class. She'd often debated whether the situation would change, and now it had – considerably. He'd invited her to this seaside resort, paying for everything down to the smallest expense.

'We're together,' he said, filling the glasses again and emptying the bottle, 'and that's the way it ought to be. I adore you,' he added with a smile.

She smiled back, suddenly tender, and put her hand over his.

'Everyone should learn from us,' he declared. 'People, Lita, are not good at loving. We're together now and when we go back we'll think it over again. You'll think about whether you want us to go on being together. I want you to be my wife.'

She agreed – agreed to the idea of thinking about it, but all she dared say was yes, of course, because she knew she had to look after him. Something told her so.

In the aseptic hotel room she tried to arouse him but to no effect. As he'd been drinking, it was easy for her to blame him, which she did without resentment. She was even tired of that.

[141]

'Why don't you read me something by Felisberto?' he said, a child asking for a bedtime story.

She began the marvellous tale about the green heart, a semiprecious stone set in a tie pin, that unleashes a train of memories in its owner. One of these involves a woman, inexplicably covered in swansdown, sitting day after day in a chair, apparently plucking something on her lap. Soon he was sleeping contentedly, with a little smile on his face. 'Thanks for introducing me to Felisberto,' he'd said to her a few days before. And how better express his gratitude, she thought, than by lying there now, sensuous lips slightly parted, bewitched, as if feather-bedecked himself, into sleep. She went on with the story until she too drifted off into the stream of free-wheeling associations that precedes slumber; she fell asleep clasping the green heart.

She dreamed she was in Mar del Plata, where her sister lived. Somehow three days had gone by, she'd not yet been to visit her, and here she was about to leave the city in twenty minutes. It was only when she decided to phone that she realized how frantic she was growing, and this was what came across to her sister. Imagine being right there and not letting her know. She was with a cousin; the return coach was to depart at any moment. How could she possibly have imagined – this made her still more frantic – that she could get to the coach station at the far side of the city in ten minutes?

She woke up thinking of the green heart. She was in a spotless hotel room, whose cold bareness cramped her imagination. From the first, she'd told him, 'It's too Franciscan. Don't you dare put away my trinkets; they help me think.' He'd immediately chortled over this; he was the last person on earth you'd ask to put anything away. He left newspapers piled all over the floor, because he couldn't be bothered to throw them out. No, her trinkets – bracelets, pendants, necklaces, rings – were meant to be left on the dressing table for her to look at as well as to be worn and to stir his thoughts. They were her green heart, she thought, looking at them.

Then the afternoon turned autumnal. They strolled in the

sun, discovering little unpaved lanes and other spots they hadn't seen before. Among the dunes, he wanted a cigarette, and they tried to talk about the future, a topic that kept intruding on their remarks about the scenery. They'd come to the next beach, an overcrowded place that catered for all types of holiday-makers. They agreed how much they loathed such resorts, but they found a twee bar, where they stopped for refreshment.

One or two eucalyptus trees and a bed of zinnias stuck out in a landscape he found bleak. 'It's stark here,' he said, and they sat down to drink and to eat shellfish under a green canvas sunshade made up of leaf shapes.

The breeze blew wisps of her hair about, and for a few seconds he tried to hold them down. He talked of finding a big old house in a residential part of Buenos Aires, Palermo say, where they could start a new life together. She believed none of it. She listened, her mind closed, thinking it was possible but he'd never be able to do it. For a moment or two she wanted to believe him but it was hopeless, her head would not obey her. She couldn't get beyond the clam he held up to her mouth or the ash he allowed to grow on his cigarette, until it could no longer support itself and like a tiny bit of pumice stone curved and floated down, dropping all by itself.

I'm going to be good, she told herself, I'm going to believe him. I have to get my life together. At which point he smiled like a schoolboy who has just played a trick, and his beautiful green eyes were blue, were green again; they held all the warmth of summer by the sea.

That evening, he got the hotel keeper's daughter to sell him wine so that he could stay on at their table after it had been cleared. He said he had to finish an article about beaches for a weekly news magazine. The girl was impressed to learn they had a writer staying at the hotel, but when he had everything he wanted within reach he wrote nothing. She felt uneasy again. She asked him if they could sleep on the beach, and they did, until the cold woke them. A night or two later, they took a coach back to the city where they lived.

The following day he ambled about the neighbourhood, while she went to work. He needed to return to normal but he found it hard to cast off the mantle of laziness that the seaside had thrown over them. After that, she wanted to be alone. The city at last forced its way into their days, filling them with stress and strain.

Late one afternoon they met again. He arrived drunk and became jealous of Juan, an old mutual friend, who saw what was going on and left. It was at her place. He wanted to talk about a plan of his, but he had already forgotten it and he kept staring at a distant light, a lamp on somebody's balcony. It seemed to bedazzle him. He asked for a glass of wine; she tried to dissuade him. Then he went to look for one in the kitchen, where he found that the distant light wouldn't leave him alone. It had followed him from the balcony, through the living-room, into the kitchen. He wanted to know what Juan had been doing there. She laughed, immediately realized this was the wrong thing to do, and pretended it was not important.

By now he was getting nasty, and his terror of the lamp dogged him wherever he turned. He looked at himself in the mirror; the light followed him. He asked her again what Juan had been up to. She didn't laugh; she said she assumed he'd come to visit her. The 'assumed' annoyed him and, blinded by the light, he threatened to hit her.

She picked up a bottle that he'd put on the table, spilling wine on the floor. He grabbed the bottle from her hand and began to chase her through the flat, until he caught her back in the kitchen. Seizing her by the hair and ramming her head against a projecting corner, he said he was going to kill her. She knew he meant it. She thought about living and made herself stand still. How could she get his mind off the sharp corner so that he hit her about the head instead? She stared into his eyes, without hatred, a victim whose only desire was to live.

That night was hell, a nightmare of evil. Afterwards, he wept, full of remorse, but soon began to blame her for everything that had happened. She wanted to live. He felt that there were things in him that she didn't understand, and again the light began to pursue him. He started throwing things, anything he could lay hands on, once more turning against her and the light. She tried to leave, to call for help. He told her that if she took a single step he'd kill her. All she wanted was to wake up alive. Once the light went away, he'd be able to sleep.

She was cleaning the floor, trying to remove all traces of the wine and his raving, when he got up. She didn't look at him but went on with what she was doing, as if he did not exist. He opened the door to go, and she felt her life coming back.

'Cheers,' he said, pulling the door shut behind him.

She heard him outside, his feet shuffling to the lift.

She had once read Flaubert's *Sentimental Education* and had found it a very fine novel, a book that taught one to hope, to be cheerful, to live. She searched for it now and, when she located her copy, swore on it that she'd never again see the man who had just left.

NEVER GO TO GENOA
IN WINTER

Rodolfo Rabanal

That winter we were poor tourists in smart places, but
mercifully in the off season the smartness lay dormant and
our poverty was not too extreme. At the time, I was sending
weekly articles to a Buenos Aires newspaper and I had a job
in Paris as a translator, so that without having to skimp or
want for anything we lived comfortably. Fed up with the
endless cold, grey Paris skies, we set off for Italy, not giving
a thought to what we would do when summer came. For the
time being, it was enough to be driving down the Ligurian
coast to Pisa with a view to spending ten days in Florence.
So, after servicing the trusty white Volkswagen I'd bought
two years before from an attractive, lonely woman in Enghien-
les-Bains, we left for Italy.

We skirted Genoa one sunlit morning, I remember, promis-
ing ourselves that we'd stay there for two or three days on the
way back. The long dark winter had drained us of all our
colour, and we found the Mediterranean glare blinding.
Marisa put flowers in her hair and rubbed a thin layer of
artificial suntan on her face. Whenever possible, we tried to
lunch alfresco and to enjoy the cold, clear end-of-March
weather as much as we could, and as we did not have a lot to
do we were almost always able to.

Before Genoa we'd stopped off in Spotorno, and I mentioned to Marisa that Lawrence and Frieda had lived there in
a little house overlooking the valley, probably on land now
taken up by the motorway, when he was entering the final

stages of tuberculosis and she was still fresh and appealing. Marisa felt sorry for Lawrence, such a good-looking young man and attractive too to judge from photographs, and I remembered a letter in which he described to a friend the slow dawn in Spotorno, with the mist rising from the valley and the first rays of sun on Frieda's head as she leaned out of the window naked.

That day we had scampi for lunch, with a light but strong rosé that looked almost red when the sun shone vertically onto it, and afterwards we had a couple of espressos laced with Sambuca. Marisa's honey-coloured hair was getting back its natural glow, and she ran her fingers through it and shook it out under the streaming midday sunlight, as we went on drinking Sambuca in stubby little glasses and talking about Lawrence and his passionate life and about the good, the magnificent good, being in Italy had done him.

Then, towards the end of the afternoon, we reached Rapallo, where we took a room with a shower in a hotel above the Gran Caffé. We were feeling the journey and the recklessness of the liqueur, and we showered and changed our clothes because we wanted to have a snoop down the *lungomare* to see what daily life in Rapallo was like – if at this time of year there was any.

Marisa kept on about Lawrence, suspecting that Frieda had wrecked him. 'I don't mean the artist,' Marisa said, 'but it does seem to me that she wrecked the man.' I wanted to know what made her think a woman could in fact wreck a man, even by loving him, and she said it sometimes happened. 'In that case,' I said, 'there must be men who can wreck a woman.' 'Of course,' she reflected, 'but I don't think that could happen quite so often.'

It was cold, but the night was bright, and the ghost of a light still shivered in the sky. The promenade was full of elderly Englishmen with brick-red faces and aged ladies wrapped in expensive furs. There were also young couples looking each other over and middle-aged people out for a good time. A trio of beautiful women came along laughing, arm in arm with a big fat man; one of the girls wore her coat unbuttoned, exposing a good part of her bosom. She could have been naked underneath the coat. The man patted her bottom and blew out smoke from a large cigar. Some violinists and a couple of trumpeters played a catchy song, '*Domani vado via*', or something of the kind, while a plump tallish woman of about sixty jigged about holding her partner's hand.

We strolled right to the far end of the promenade, where the marina breakwater began and the market square opened out, but by now it was dark, the stalls were closed, and it was no longer possible to see the boats or the sea or to appreciate the deep pink of the old buildings. We walked over cold, damp cobbles, sniffing the pungent smell of fish, and we decided to go back to the Gran Caffè, which, it seemed, was the best place on the *lungomare*. We ordered some sandwiches of crusty bread and spicy Italian ham, and we asked for a carafe of the rosé we had drunk at midday in Spotorno. We toasted someone or other – I don't remember whom, probably ourselves.

Marisa's hands were red with cold, but her cheeks and forehead had begun to glow with a healthy tan. Her bright, laughing eyes reflected the exhaustion of the long day and showed a trace of the abandon that wine brings on. The tables were filling up. A couple seated not far from us was arguing in English. We could not follow what they were saying, but their tone was heated, and it wasn't hard to tell that it was the final tiresome stage of a long lovers' tiff. Despite the man's imploring look, the woman refused to meet his eyes. He was clearly inventing lame excuses. His manner was cautious and pained, then blinkered and almost violent, yet he kept his voice down; he was aware that this passionate scene was a private matter which didn't deserve a public airing.

'They must be Americans,' Marisa remarked. 'She's beautiful and he's handsome.'

Marisa was always finding something handsome in men who seemed to me past their best. This one revealed an intensity that contrasted with the woman's almost bloodless Nordic beauty. Her thick ash-blonde hair fell to her shoulders in soft, graceful curls. Impeccably dressed in a blue skirt, she wore over it a fine black fur that served to set off a gleaming head of hair. She could not have been more than thirty. The couple's savoir faire and determination to keep up appearances were plain, for at one point she looked at him with the unmistakable intention of insulting him but in view of where they were she chose to check the impulse and instead turned towards the street, where a pretty young prostitute was passing by with an enormous St Bernard. From one of the tables someone called out to her, '*Fortuna, Fortuna, vieni a mangiare!*' Now the American fell to pleading again. He must have been about fifty and, with his grizzled brown beard and sad, damp, sandy moustache, looked like an ageing young man. He was very tall and thin, and every time he began to speak he leaned over the table, his large, slender hands continually playing with the rims of the wineglasses in movements that kept holding back an urge to reach out and snatch the woman from wherever she was. They had been drinking liqueurs and afterwards what might have been gin or vodka, and he went on drinking until he lost his poise; he was trying to get moral support from something that did not seem to be there. Clearly seething inside, he was on the point of burning up completely when he knocked over one of the glasses that cluttered the table and it fell and broke into smithereens. He started to apologize in terrible Italian, while she, aware that everyone was watching them, could not control a sudden quivering of her eyelids and her stiffened lips.

'Good Lord,' murmured Marisa, 'they're going to go for each other.'

She was now looking straight at him, laying into him, but nobody could make out what cruel, withering things she was saying. The man was clearly about to break down, and she, despite her coolness, to lose her precious composure. Then all at once she fell drily silent and turned towards the street again, her eyes fixed on something there, while he, desperately wanting those eyes on him, clutched at the sleeve of her fur coat. On the other side of the wooden flower boxes bordering

the pavement a young man in jeans and suede jacket slouched
by casting eager, furtive glances towards the Americans' table,
at which point the blonde – what could her name have been?
– seemed to respond anxiously, although we couldn't be sure
of this. Anyway, she managed to remove the man's hand from
her arm, lifting it firmly, the way you lift the hand of a sleeping
child and tuck it under the blankets – albeit without the same
tenderness. And then she got up and made her way between
the chairs and tables and out into the street, quickly, haughtily,
in embarrassment. But the young man in the suede jacket,
whoever he was, had vanished.

Mortified and tearful, the American spread his hands out
among the debris on the table, an unlit cigarette in his fingers.
A second later, searching in the pockets of his long white
mackintosh, he took out a handful of lire, put the money on
the table, and staggered out. In the street he collected himself
and set off trying to walk in a straight line. He was extremely
drunk.

The fat man and the beautiful girls whom we'd seen
strolling along the promenade reappeared and they all sat
down at the table the couple had just left. For a moment or
two the man's sheer bulk made even more insubstantial the
ghost of the now absent American. These people were coarse
vaudeville actors occupying a stage that wasn't theirs. 'What
a pig!' said Marisa. The girl in the open coat went on exposing
her mother-of-pearl breasts, which were as beautiful and pale
as her features were splendidly vulgar.

A strange unease woke me sometime in the early hours of that
night. Silence reigned, and the sea could be heard on the beach.
I did not realize at once that Marisa was not in the bed. I
opened the doors onto the balcony to see if she were there –
which was absurd, for it was cold – and, shutting them quickly,
I turned on the light and went to the bathroom. There was
Marisa, seated on the lavatory lid, smoking, a coat round her
shoulders and her cheeks pale and drawn. 'Don't kiss me,' she

said, 'I'm about to throw up the whole of Liguria. I don't think Italy agrees with me tonight, and I wish I were at home.' 'Where exactly?' I asked. There was Paris, with the old lime-trees along the Avenue Bosquet and, before that, Calle Bulnes, in Buenos Aires. 'At home,' Marisa said again. We had a bottle of surgical spirits in one of our cases. Fetching it, I told her to inhale, then I shook out a handkerchief, dampened it with the alcohol, and she applied it like a compress to her stomach. She looked at herself in the bathroom mirror and sighed in disgust at her reflection. 'God, what a sight!' In the dim, uriney light of that antiquated bathroom in an old Italian hotel my heroine must have felt bedraggled; her damp locks were plastered to her temples. 'If ever we split up,' she said, 'please don't make scenes that will humiliate us for ever.' 'Right,' I said, 'we'll do it cheerfully.' At least I managed to make her smile, and I poured half a finger of Sambuca into the tooth mug on the bathroom shelf. Italy was turning me into an alcoholic.

We went back to the creaking bed that sagged in the middle and was now as cold as the rest of the room, since the heating had gone off while we were asleep. It was beginning to grow light, and Marisa muttered something about crude pleasure-mongers in a decadent world and poor, handsome Englishmen punished by love's cruelty. She was a bit over the top, and I supposed it was because she was feeling bilious so I agreed, but I was dropping off. Tomorrow, I thought – today rather – we'll be in Florence.

On our way through Carrara we found out that there was a hotel caterers' strike in Florence, which involved pickets. We spent three uncomfortable days amid riotous crowds and dirty streets. They were burning refuse on the banks of the Arno and had hung a cardboard phallus on the David. All we could find was expensive sanctuary in the Montebello Hotel, with its bed as big as a summer alfalfa field and its interminable breakfasts. In the Caffé Rivoire we had a surprise. We thought we saw our American friend thrown headlong into the mud among a gang of revellers, but it turned out to be someone

[151]

who looked like him. We left Florence after four days, feeling that Italy was playing tricks on us.

A little later, now on our way back to France, we stopped in Genoa. Our resources were running out, and, on the advice of someone in the tourist office, we chose a modest hotel. 'A good, cheap place,' she told us. She was right about the latter. The hotel faced the ancient, dark, dilapidated palazzi of the Piazza Nunziata, behind the port but in its immediate vicinity; it had noisy, theatrical, neighbours. These, who were not so much poor as classless and ostentatiously down at heel, had a picaresque air that was as comical as it was disturbing, particularly after dark. Down one side of the hotel ran a narrow passageway, barely as wide as a small car – a red-light district, as they say – a *vicoletto* riddled with dens of prostitution, the girls in the port all day long, tarted up as if for the stage and on defiant offer from a little before midday.

We consoled ourselves that all was real, alive, healthy – Genoa, the ramshackle matrix of the Americas, the unlikely cradle of Columbus. In short, we grasped at these secondary considerations, to which, I must confess, Marisa gave in not without some resistance. Our room, which directly overlooked the alleyway, had such a sloped floor that it was like a ship on the high seas. There was a wardrobe with a mirror, a chipped enamel wash basin, and an iron bedstead painted a bluish green. The bathroom had a shower, but if we turned it full on – which was not saying much – we drenched the floor by the bed. Luckily, there were no fleas or other bugs. Luckily, we decided to make ourselves comfortable and, as best we could, enjoy the extravagant atmosphere.

At night, if we opened the window, odd snatches of music came from the slum neighbourhood below – waterfront *cumbias,* Italian rock, and European tango – as well as the pungent smell from someone's kitchen, probably the hotel's, whose dining-room in fact wasn't too bad and even had a piano for anyone who wanted to show off his talents.

And, sitting at the piano, there he was. At first we hardly recognized him. A table lamp with an opaque white globe gave off a dim, watery light over the keys only, leaving the pianist's face in shadow. It was our second night in Genoa, and we were eating stew with the odd piece of veal in it; all the rest was pleasant and even the veal itself had its points. Ever faithful, we stuck to our Ligurian wine, and I looked forward to an espresso with my dose of Sambuca. There were fewer diners, and the service, which was good, was presided over by a brilliantined head waiter whom everyone called Signor Peduzzi. Marisa summoned Signor Peduzzi to ask if the pianist would play 'Lady Be Good'. Peduzzi said he would be delighted to ask although he must explain that the pianist was not a professional hired by the management but a guest, 'An American, signora, who is a bit . . .' – and still baring his big crooked yellow teeth in a smile, he put a finger to his temple. Peduzzi looked a lot like a waiter by the name of Domingo at the Tortoni back in Buenos Aires – the same big, crooked, yellow teeth, the same voracious but tired grin. Peduzzi hid a deep-seated bitterness behind effusive southern Italian courtesy. Underneath he was as gloomy and decrepit as Genoa itself and, in many ways, as dark and forbidding as the Tortoni.

The American had a glass of whisky on the piano lid and he sipped it deliberately, carefully, all the while running the fingers of his free hand over the white notes in a subtle improvisation which he used as a bridge to move from one number to the next while he bent his elbow. Then he played 'Lady Be Good'. When he finished, Marisa clapped gratefully, and he got up from the stool and took a bow like a stage performer, with a slight nod. That was when we knew for sure that he was the man from Rapallo, part of our sleepless night, along with the vomiting and the surgical spirits on Marisa's delicious blonde belly. He was dressed in a light tobacco-coloured corduroy jacket, grey flannel trousers that were too big for him, and a black polo-necked sweater.

He went straight back to the keys and, after a pause for whisky, began to play something that turned into 'As Time Goes By', which he did very well, swathing it in pure nostalgia and melancholy, so much so that Marisa, ever susceptible to a tug at the heartstrings, felt for my hand with hers among the plates of cold stew, cups, napkins, and the empty dish of what had been a salad of basil, tomatoes, and sliced mozzarella sprinkled with oregano and thyme.

The American seemed clean and in good form, but when he came over to our table to say hello, introducing himself a touch nervously as Mr Robert Kemble, from Boston – 'but in fact now resident in New York, though not of late' – we could see that in places his jacket was threadbare and newly stained by wine or food. Or maybe both. His dark-grey eyes were reddened by alcohol or tears, and perhaps also by smoke and uncertainty, and the hand holding the glass had a slight case of the shakes. From a step or two behind him Peduzzi gave us a look to suggest that the man was not part of the programme, and it seemed to me that the waiter shook his dark slick head in resignation.

I savoured my Sambuca and prepared not to worry. Mr Kemble explained to Marisa in a mixture of languages – mainly a mannered basic English – that he wasn't really a musician but that '*Lady Be Good*' was an old passion of his and always seemed to him in the nature of a plea for love on the part of a suffering lover, which, as it turned out, was more or less the story of his life.

Then he tossed back the remains of his glass of whisky and asked for his bottle, begging us to join him with whatever we fancied. I said I was drinking Sambuca, and he approved but without much conviction. Marisa asked for a cognac, and Kemble began to regale us with the story of his love affair and breakup, citing the beautiful woman we'd seen in Rapallo, Catherine Brett, I think he said – Catherine something, anyway – sandwiched between half-uttered abuse and apologies: '*Ah, signora . . . io voglio . . .* I mean . . .'

A storm of incomprehensible words followed these mumblings. The people at the next table began to stare. A fat man, who had just sat back replete and lit a cigar, said something to his companion. She nodded, her lower jaw sinking into the soft roundness of her double chin, and as she did so I noticed a frown of disapproval that may not have been restricted to Kemble. The man smiled without removing his cigar, while she, grand as a dowager, glared at our table.

Despite her embarrassment, Marisa was trying to be kind to Kemble. Since Rapallo, she had taken the American's side and was clearly predisposed to show him sympathy and tolerance. A loser is always more attractive than a winner, and anyone could see that Kemble belonged to the former category, with his young man's ravaged face and his look of a Bostonian gone to the dogs. Meanwhile, how were we to cut short his brittle, plaintive harangue, delivered with a sarcastic smile which countered tears and perhaps held back a full outburst?

I had the impression that all Kemble wanted was for the absent Catherine Brett to see him again, even if the look she gave him were a sentence of death. He had poured himself another whisky, and then I saw that Signor Peduzzi was muttering to the imposing lady at the next table, after which he came over to us. Kemble saw too and he made some obscene remark about Peduzzi, but the head waiter touched the American's shoulder and asked him if he would mind moving off. Peduzzi had polished manners, I must admit. Kemble went on talking, and I wanted him to leave gracefully. I realized that I was asking too much too soon.

'This man is not making trouble,' Marisa protested, sticking to the logic of her first feelings. Ever affable, Peduzzi said that the hotel could not allow anyone to annoy the guests and, 'unfortunately, signora, there have been one or two complaints.' Then, his old democratic dignity stirring, Kemble stood up and began to abuse him. '*Va bene*,' said Peduzzi, '*va bene*.' Kemble was now swearing, labelling Genoa and all Italy 'a corrupt cradle of fascists and thieves disguised as head waiters.' Grave, yet smiling his broad, voracious but tired grin, Peduzzi took Kemble by the lapels, meaning to shove him out of the dining-room. Our distinguished jilted drunk shook Peduzzi off with a brusque movement of his arms without the

[155]

Italian's losing his brilliantined composure or his swift hotel manager's reflexes.

'*Dino, eh, Dino! Presto!*' he called.

Dino must have rushed out of the kitchen, because a white napkin was still draped over his unusually broad shoulders. He was a barrel of a man of about six foot four, with huge fists like cobblestones and eyes like tiny grey glass marbles.

'We can't have people walking in here insulting us!' our monumental lady at the next table said, giving vent to her indignation.

Dino took hold of Kemble and, when he resisted, bent the American's arm up behind his back. Poor Kemble let out the cry he'd been holding back until that moment, but he was still able to summon up the strength to land Dino a left that caught one of his broad cheekbones, after which Dino was obliged to flatten Kemble's nose, releasing an immediate jet of pure Boston blood. At that, Marisa could restrain herself no longer and began to rail against the brute and call the hotel staff a pack of savage murderers. My only course was to get up and intercede with Peduzzi on the grounds that this violence was quite out of proportion to anything the poor man had done. I said, morever – foolishly, I admit – that something had happened to Kemble in Rapallo that –

'That what?' Peduzzi interrupted. 'Something happened to me in Rapallo too, signore, and in Rome and in Naples. Is there anyone to whom something hasn't happened somewhere?'

He was quite right. Something was happening to me too that night in Genoa. Marisa had given me a stony look which, without daring to say I should have in some way intervened, was full of reproach. In my view that was absurd.

'The fact is . . .' I muttered, but Peduzzi had already moved off, making his automatic bow and ushering in the two elderly musicians in evening dress we had seen the night before and who now launched into a gloomy rendering of '*La vie en rose*'.

'I need a stiff drink,' Marisa announced, her eyes glued to the tablecloth. I called the waiter, who topped up my liverish

Fury's brandy, and I filled my small glass with another dollop of Sambuca. I was at the point of losing my temper as I anticipated the inconsiderate demands that Marisa's romantic indignation might make on me, when I hit on the solution of getting drunk enough to sink into a leaden slumber. But just as I was preparing for a disastrous breach between us, she surprised me by suddenly reaching for my hand. Good, so maybe after all she wasn't head over heels in love with that clown of a Kemble, in which case how stupid I'd been to sully her pure humanitarian feelings with my nasty suspicions. And how selfish I was being in view of poor Kemble's calamity.

Reassured, I called Peduzzi over. He was terribly solicitous, and I asked after *il povero signor americano*, suggesting that he might need help and that a doctor be called. Peduzzi smiled broadly and told me not to worry, because Mr Kemble was in good hands. I asked what that meant, and, lowering his voice Peduzzi said, '*L'abbiamo gettato nel vicolo delle puttane, signore. Sì, per farlo consolare.*'

The brothel – they'd thrown him to the whores for consolation. 'And why not, signore? We are a Christian people, and after the beating Mr Kemble deserved a bit of consolation. *Sì, signore*, firmness and mercy.'

The two old musicians had begun to play – with neither firmness nor mercy – '*Three Coins in the Fountain*', with tarantella variations. Our buxom neighbour had cuddled up all lovey-dovey beside her brawny lover like some sated wild animal. He had put one claw on the back of her neck and with a finger was twisting her black-dyed hair behind her ear. Marisa wept, but with laughter. Or maybe it was the other way round. Her face had gone redder, as if heated by a bonfire. I supposed she had drunk too much, but I had too, so my point of view was scarcely reliable. We went to bed anxious. I dreamed of brothels and fat women, but if Marisa dreamed I have no idea what about. The next morning we decided to leave.

It was early when we came down to breakfast, and the kitchen floor smelled of pine disinfectant. The waiter who served us looked sleepy. Peduzzi was nowhere to be seen, and I pictured him snoring away in a high, old-fashioned, narrow bed, his tinted hair tied up in a hairnet. We breakfasted in silence on black coffee and toast and still without a word put our suitcases in the car. Robert Kemble sat at a window that looked out onto the piazza, but he was not alone. The woman wore the same sumptuous black fur she had worn that night in Rapallo, but now instead of a blue skirt she wore jeans. By day she gave off a tired pallor; she seemed more beautiful than I remembered, and her blonde hair caught the wan light that came in from the street. Kemble, a glass of gin in one hand, was going on and on at her. He had a plaster above his right eye and the other was black and blue. I did not see whether his nose showed any damage, but some haemostatic ointment had been put on a cut on his chin. The blonde beauty stirred her *cappuccino* and stared off into a world beyond him. As we passed we said hello, but Kemble glanced at us mechanically, his look vague and troubled, without the slightest sign of recognition. He was evidently busy inventing lame excuses and, his overbearing voice accompanied by imploring gestures, working up impossible accusations.

We left Italy, and on the way through Saint-Paul de Vence I was about to say to Marisa, 'This is where Lawrence died.' Instead, I said nothing. Marisa was asleep, her head tilted back against the top of the seat.

Notes on contributors

ENRIQUE BUTTI, born in Santa Fe in 1949, is the author of the comic novel, *Aiaiay* (1986) and a novel for teenagers *No me digan que no* (1989). He has also written plays and a study of the Santa Fe poet José Pedroni, *Del nombrar y de los nombres* (1989). A student of cinema at the University of the Litoral in his native city until 1972, he went on with the aid of Rotary Club scholarships to specialize at the Centro Sperimentale di Cinematografia, in Rome, where he directed short films, worked as an animator, and wrote film reviews for *Bianco & Nero*. He also studied the Italian language and literature at the Università per Stranieri, at Perugia. His first stories appeared in *Tiempo Argentino*, in Buenos Aires, and in *El Litoral*, in Santa Fe, the newspaper he joined when he returned to Argentina in 1983 and where he still works. On a Fulbright fellowship in 1990 he spent several months in Iowa City as part of the International Writing Program. That same year *Aiaiay* was published in an Italian translation. His story here is as yet unpublished in Spanish and marks his first appearance in English.

HUMBERTO COSTANTINI was born in Buenos Aires in 1924 and died there in 1987. His passions – apart from his family – were literary artistry and social justice, and in both spheres he was an ardent polemicist. Quite early on, with his first stories about everyday people from the unfashionable neighbourhoods of Buenos Aires, he gained a devoted following and became influential among younger writers. In 1976, shortly after the establishment of what turned out to be an unspeakably brutal military takeover of the country, Costantini fled to Mexico to save his life, only returning to Argentina early in 1984 after the restoration of civilian rule. His short fiction appeared in several volumes, some of it overlapping from book to book. These collections were: *De por aquí nomás* (1958); *Un señor alto, rubio, de bigotes* (1963); *Una vieja historia de caminantes* (1967), which contained seven new pieces and reprinted eleven others from the previous collections, together with two monologues from the book called *Tres monólogos* (1964); *Háblenme de Funes* (1970); *Libro de Trelew* (1973) *Bandeo* (1975); and *En la noche* (1985). The Mexican edition of *Háblenme de Funes* (1980) also reprinted the stories from *Bandeo,* together with a new story 'La llegada'. In exile Costantini also wrote two novels. The first, *De Dioses, hombrecitos y policías*, was published in 1979 in Mexico and in Cuba, where it won the important Casa de las Américas Prize. This made the author instantly famous, and his book was translated into nine languages. It appeared in English in New York as *The Gods, the Little Guys and the Police* (1984). The second novel, *La larga noche de Francisco Sanctis* (1984), was published on his return to Buenos Aires, appearing in New York in 1985 and in London in 1987 under the title *The Long Night of Francisco Sanctis*. The last book published in his lifetime was *¡Chau, Pericles!* (1986), his collected theatre, which included a play for children and reprinted the earlier monologues. Costantini was also a poet. His first collection, *Cuestiones con la vida* (1966), was reissued in successively enlarged editions in 1970, 1976, 1982 (in Mexico), and 1986. The poems of *Más cuestiones con la vida* (1974) were incorporated into subsequent editions of the former. One of his plays and several stories, including the one published here, won prizes in Mexico; both his 1967 and 1970 story collections won municipal prizes of the City of Buenos Aires. Costantini's short fiction appeared in many anthologies and in such literary magazines as *Polémica Literaria, Mar Dulce, Propósitos, Davar, Aporte, Nueva Expresión,* and *Gaceta Literaria,* which he helped edit. He had also been one of the founders of *El Grillo de Papel* (The Paper Cricket) and *El Escarabajo de Oro* (The Gold Bug). For years before his exile he earned his living in scientific research as a technician in a laboratory largely concerned with veterinary medicine, and in this capacity he even wrote several technical papers. After 1976, he lived by his pen. On his death he left some 400-odd pages of a very long, unfinished novel, *La rapsodia de Raquel Liberman,* the story of a ring of Polish-Jewish pimps and whores in Argentina during the 1920s. Costantini was of Italian Sephardic Jewish origin.

JOSÉ PABLO FEINMANN, the son of a Catholic mother and Jewish father, was born in Buenos Aires in 1943 and, as an author, has enjoyed a prolific, threefold career as novelist, essayist, and writer of film scripts. His four novels are *Últimos días de la víctima* (1979), *Ni el tiro del final* (1981), *El ejército de ceniza* (1986), and *La astucia de la razón* (1990). The first and third of these are soon to appear in French. His six volumes of essays on Argentine politics and the history of Argentine thought include *El peronismo y la primacia de la política* (1974); *Filosofía y Nación* (1982); *Estudios sobre el peronismo* (1983), a re-working of the material in his first book; *El mito del eterno fracaso* (1985); *La creación de lo posible* (1986); and *López Rega, la cara oscura de Perón* (1987). To date, nine of his scripts have been made into films, including a version of his first novel; three of these screenplays have been published together as *Escritos para el cine* (1988). A Licentiate in Philosophy of the University of Buenos Aires since 1969, he taught the subject at the university between 1968 and 1975 and currently lectures on contemporary philosophy (Hegel, in whom he is a specialist, Marx, Sartre, etc.) at a school of journalism. He also contributes to the literary pages of the newspaper *Clarín* and from 1982-89 wrote a column for the magazine *Humor.* Feinmann is married to the cinema art director and costume designer María Julia Bertotto. His short story here, which is still unpublished in Spanish, is his first appearance in English.

[161]

JUAN FORN is the author of the novel *Corazones cautivos más arriba* (1987) and the short stories *Nadar de noche* (1991), from which the present story is drawn. In 1979 and 1981, he published small volumes of five and fifteen poems, respectively. He has also compiled a volume of *Conversaciones con Enrique Pinti* (1990), the Argentine comedian. Born in Buenos Aires in 1959, Forn was educated at Cardinal Newman, a private school run by Irish Christian Brothers. He has lived in Europe for a year, where he taught football in Paris as a coach in an elementary school, and has worked as a ghost writer of commercial fiction, historical novels, and how-to books. He has also written two film scripts, one a musical for a rock group. From 1984 to 1989 he was employed by the Buenos Aires publisher Emecé as a literary editor and translator. In 1991 he became Editor in Chief at Editorial Planeta. An anthology of Argentine short fiction, edited by him, appeared in Spain in 1991. This is his first work to come out in English.

RODRIGO FRESÁN was forced to leave Buenos Aires with his parents at the age of ten (he was born there in 1963) to go and live in Venezuela, which at the time enjoyed a healthier political climate. His high-school studies completed, he returned to Argentina in 1979, where he has since worked as a comic-strip artist, then in an advertising agency, and subsequently as a journalist on a variety of newspapers and magazines. Having also done a year of military service, he is currently deputy literary editor of *Pagina/12* and an editor and writer on *Cuisine & Vins,* where he contributes pieces on tourism and on the gastronomic side of literature. His fiction has appeared in both these periodicals as well as in the monthly *El Porteño.* Fresán is the author of *Historia argentina* (1991), a volume of connected stories, which became a best-seller. His story here, his first appearance in English, is from that volume. Presently at work on a novel, he is on the verge of marrying the actress Claudia Gallegos.

JUAN JOSÉ HERNÁNDEZ was born in 1932 in northern Argentina, in Tucumán, the smallest of the country's provinces. A student of literature at the universities of Córdoba and Buenos Aires, he later worked for twenty-three years as a journalist on an important Buenos Aires newspaper, during which time he contributed stories, poems, and reviews to *Sur, La Nación*, and *La Gaceta de Tucumán*. To date, he has published three volumes of poetry, *Negada permanencia y La siesta y la naranja* (1952), *Claridad vencida* (1957), and *Otro verano* (1966); a novel, *Ciudad de los sueños* (1971); and three collections of short stories, *Dos narraciones* (1963), *El inocente* (1965), and *La favorita* (1977). A selection of stories from the last two was made by the author and published under the title *Cuentos* in 1986; it included one new story, written that same year, the tale chosen for this anthology. Hernández's stories have been widely anthologized in Latin America and abroad, and translations of them have appeared in the United States, France, Sweden, and Germany. His work has also won important prizes, including a First Municipal Prize for fiction, in 1966, and a National Prize for fiction, in 1981. Awarded a Guggenheim Fellowship in 1969, he currently conducts a writer's workshop in poetry and fiction. He has translated (with Eduardo Paz Leston) a volume of Tennessee Williams's poems.

SYLVIA IPARRAGUIRRE has a degree in literature from the University of Buenos Aires, where she later studied towards a doctorate in linguistics. As a member of the Argentine research institute CONICET, which she joined in 1981, she has worked in sociolinguistics, dialects, and the indigenous languages of the Argentine. In 1970, she met the writer Abelardo Castillo, whom she married in 1976. With him and others she founded the literary magazine *El Ornitorrinco* (The Duck-billed Platypus), a successor to *El Escarabajo de Oro* (The Gold Bug), to which she had been a contributor. Since 1985, she has also taught at the Latin American Institute of the University of Buenos Aires. She was born in Junín, in the Province of Buenos Aires, in 1947. Her fiction and essays have appeared in several anthologies and in *Clarín, Página/12, Contexto, Puro Cuento,* and *Cuadernos Hispanomericanos.* This, her first work to appear in English, is from her story collection *En el invierno de las ciudades* (1988), which won a First Municipal Prize for Fiction. A new book of stories, *Probables lluvias por la noche* is scheduled for publication in 1992. She is currently writing a novel about the three Fuegian Indians taken to London by Captain FitzRoy in the early part of the last century.

VLADY KOCIANCICH studied literature under Jorge Luis Borges at the University of Buenos Aires. For a long period, until 1973, she conducted a book program on Radio Municipal and afterwards worked for five years as a reporter for tourist magazines, during which time she travelled to most corners of the globe. She has published three novels, *La octava maravilla* (1982), *Últimos días de William Shakespeare* (1984), and *Abisinia* (1985). The first has additionally appeared in Spain and in Italian and German versions. The second, which came out in London in 1990 as *The Last Days of William Shakespeare,* has also been published in the United States and been translated into Italian, German, French, Swedish, and Norwegian. *Abisinia* has been translated into Portuguese, in Brazil, and French, in Canada. Kociancich has two story collections, *Coraje* (1969) and *Todos los caminos* (1991). Her tale here is from the latter volume, which won a prize in Spain in 1990 and whose title story won the Jorge Luis Borges Prize in Buenos Aires in 1988. Born in that city in 1941, she presently writes articles on literary subjects for *Diario 16* in Madrid. Her new novel, *Los bajos del temor,* will be published in Spain in 1992.

ALEJANDRO MANARA, born in Buenos Aires in 1954, graduated in Latin American studies from Kings College, London, in 1976, after which he travelled in the Far East. He has lived in England, Spain, Italy, and Japan, where he taught Spanish and Italian privately and in schools. Now in Argentina, he has published translations into Spanish of the Robert Louis Stevenson-Henry James correspondence and the Italo Svevo-James Joyce letters, is completing a novel, and is shortly to publish a volume of his minimalist short fiction, a few examples of which have appeared in the Buenos Aires newspaper *Página/12*. 'Domesticity', Manara's first work to appear in English, is still unpublished in Spanish. He currently contributes twice a month on literary subjects to another Buenos Aires paper, *El Cronista*.

DANIEL MOYANO was born in Buenos Aires in 1930 and, orphaned at the age to six, went to live near the city of Córdoba, which he left in 1960 to settle in La Rioja, in the northwest of Argentina. There, as a violist, he both taught at the conservatory and played in its string quartet and chamber orchestra; at the same time, as a journalist, he was a founder of *El Independiente* and also a correspondent for the Buenos Aires newspaper *Clarín*. After being briefly jailed during the military takeover in 1976, Moyano left with his family to take up residence in Madrid. (His account of this affair, in Andrew Graham-Yooll's *After the Despots* [1991], is obligatory reading.) In 1981, he received Spanish nationality. Moyano's literary production to date (variously first published in Córdoba [Argentina], Buenos Aires, Caracas, Madrid, and Barcelona) consists of six novels and six story collections. The former are: *Una luz muy lejana* (1967), *El oscuro* (1968), *El Trino del Diablo* (1974), *El vuelo del tigre* (1981), *Libro de navíos y borrascas* (1983), and *Tres golpes de timbal* (1989). The latter are: *Artistas de variedades* (1960), *El rescate* (1963), *La lombriz* (1964), *El fuego interrumpido* (1967), *Mi música es para esta gente* (1970), and *El estuche de cocodrilo* (1974). *El*

Trino del Diablo y otras modulaciones is a 1988 reissue of the novel together with five new stories. There have also been two selections of stories, *El monstruo y otros cuentos* (1967) and *La espera y otros cuentos* (1978). Three of the novels have been translated into French, a book of stories into Polish, and *The Devil's Trill* appeared in London in 1989, while individual tales have been widely anthologized. Since living in Europe, Moyano has lectured on literature and conducted writing workshops in Spain, France, the United States, and Mexico. His fiction has won a number of awards – among them, the prestigious Juan Rulfo prize – and in 1970 he was made a Guggenheim Fellow. The story by him in this book is as yet unpublished in Spanish.

ELVIRA ORPHÉE, the novelist and short story writer, was born in Tucumán in 1930 and has lived in Buenos Aires for many years. Her fiction, criticism, and reviews have featured in virtually all the magazines and newspapers of note in Argentine – *Sur, La Nación, La Gaceta de Tucumán, La Prensa, Clarín, Cultura, Tiempo Argentino,* etc. – and in many others throughout Latin America. Orphée has studied literature at the universities of Buenos Aires and Rome and at the Sorbonne. In 1962–63 she worked in Paris as a reader for Gallimard. During the years preceding and following the military dictatorship in Argentina, she went to live in Caracas, where she remained from 1974 to 1981. In 1988, she was made a Guggenheim Fellow. Her six novels are *Dos veranos* (1956), *Uno* (1961), *Aire tan dulce* (1966), *En el fondo* (1969), *La última conquista de El Ángel* (1977), and *La muerte y los desencuentros* (1990); and her three story collections are *Su demonio preferido* (1973), *Las viejas fantasiosas* (1981), and *Ciego del cielo* (1991). Her fifth novel was published in New York in 1985 as *El Angel's Last Conquest.* Her story here is taken from her second collection. She has three daughters with the painter Miguel Ocampo.

MARIO PAOLETTI, poet, short story writer, and novelist, has lived in Spain since 1980, working in Toledo as director of the José Ortega y Gasset Foundation's Centre for International Studies. His literary work includes the story collections *Treblinka en Liniers y otros cuentos* (1975) – his only book to appear in Buenos Aires – and *Dos cuentos de Buenos Aires* (1981); *¡Qué aparezcan!* (1982), a portfolio of drawings and poems produced in collaboration with Charles Lantero; the poetry collections *Poemas con Arlt* (1983) and *Inventario* (1991); and a novel, *Antes del Diluvio* (1989). Born in Buenos Aires in 1940, Paoletti went to live from 1960 to 1978 in the poor northwestern Argentine province of La Rioja, where he became deputy editor of *El Independiente*, a daily newspaper run as a cooperative by journalists and print workers. While there he was jailed for four years – in his own words, 'held without charges or trial as an "ideological delinquent" ' – by the Videla dictatorship. Trained as a teacher (he also has a degree in journalism and, from the University of Córdoba, one in modern literature), Paoletti has lectured on Latin American writers in many places in Argentina and in Spain. His career in journalism began as a humourist with contributions to the magazine *Tía Vicenta*; after that he wrote for *Siete Días* and *Panorama,* in Buenos Aires, and for the Rioja magazines *El Champi* and *Proceso*. In Spain he has been a regular contributor to *Cuadernos Hispanoamericanos, Leviatán, Argumentos, El Socialista,* and the *Revista de Occidente*. His fiction, poetry, and journalism have won him prizes in his native country as well as in Spain, Cuba, and the United States. The story printed here, adapted by the author from an unpublished novel, is his first appearance in English.

RODOLFO RABANAL studied philosophy and law at the universities of Buenos Aires and La Plata before he turned to journalism, working as columnist, editor, and correspondent for dailies and weeklies such as *Clarín, Primera Plana, Ámbito Financiero, El Periodista*, and *El Expreso*. He still contributes to a wide variety of journals, including *La Nación, Panorama, Gente,* and *Somos,* in Buenos Aires, and *ABC* and the EFE agency, in Madrid. His chief literary work has been as a novelist, although he began by writing poetry and his first published book was a slim volume of verse, *Improntus* (1967). His novels are: *El apartado* (1975); *Un día perfecto* (1978); *En otra parte* (1982), made up of the short novels *Nueva York es un nervio desnudo* and *Días de gloria en Medora; El pasajero* (1984); and *El factor sentimental* (1990). His story in this anthology, his first work to appear in English, is the title piece from his small collection *No vayas a Génova en invierno* (1988). He has also written the script for the film *Gombrowicz, o la seducción* (1987) and published a children's story *Noche en Gondwana* (1988). On a Fulbright to the United States in 1979, Rabanal spent five months in Iowa City and another four in New York. He also worked in Paris from 1981 to 1984 as a cultural adviser to the French government. In 1988 he was awarded a Guggenheim Fellowship and the next year he held the position of Under-Secretary of Culture in the Alfonsín government. He was born in Buenos Aires in 1940.

ANA MARÍA SHUA was born in Buenos Aires in 1952 and studied literature at the University of Buenos Aires, from which she graduated in 1973. She has worked as an advertising copywriter, a free-lance journalist, and a film-script writer. An early starter, she published her first book, a volume of poetry, *El sol y yo* (1967), at the age of fifteen. It won two prizes. Since then, she has also published two novels – both of which have been made into films – *Soy paciente* (1980) and *Los amores de Laurita* (1984); two story collections, *Los días de pesca* (1981) and *Viajando se conoce gente* (1988); and a volume of short prose pieces, *La sueñera* (1984). *La batalla entre los elefantes y los cocodrilos* (1988), *Expedición al Amazonas* (1988), and *La fábrica del terror* (1990) are her published children's books; a fourth, *La puerta para salir del mundo,* is scheduled to appear early in 1992. Her latest volume is a selection of her magazine pieces, *El marido argentino promedio* (1991). Her stories have been chosen for anthologies in Canada, Holland, Spain, and the United States. The one in this book is from a long work in progress and is the author's second appearance in English.

MARCIAL SOUTO has published two collections of his own short story/prose pieces (*Para bajar a un pozo de estrellas* [1983] and *Trampas para pesadillas* [1988]) and compiled a half dozen or so anthologies of science fiction and what is known in the River Plate as *literatura fantástica*. At the same time, he has edited two magazines, *Minotauro* (1983–87) and *El Péndulo* (1979 to date), while also working as a free-lance editor for several different Buenos Aires publishers. His prize-winning translations from the English include fifteen books by such authors as J. G. Ballard, Ambrose Bierce, Ray Bradbury, Cordwainer Smith, and so forth. Born in 1947, in La Coruña, Spain, Souto arrived in Montevideo at the age of fourteen and lived there between 1961 and 1973 before moving to Buenos Aires. His story here comes from his second collection. Until now he has been unpublished in English.

ALICIA STEIMBERG is the author of five novels (*Músicos y relojeros* [1971]; *La Loca 101* [1973]; *Su espíritu inocente* [1981]; *El árbol del placer* [1986]; and *Amatista* [1989]) and a volume of short stories (*Como todas las mañanas* [1983]), all published in Buenos Aires, save the erotic novel *Amatista,* which appeared in Barcelona in Tusquet's famed *Sonrisa vertical* series. Her story in this anthology is from her 1983 collection and is her second appearance in English. Born in Buenos Aires in 1933, a descendent of the earliest Jewish immigrants to Argentina in the last century, she graduated in English from the Instituto Nacional del Profesorado en Lenguas Vivas. She taught English at the University of Buenos Aires from 1961 to 1966 and currently teaches the language privately. She has also worked as a professional translator (books by Isaac Bashevis Singer, Raymond Chandler, James Hadley Chase, and so forth) for a number of Argentine publishers. Her latest work is *El mundo no es de polenta* (1991), a cookery book for teenagers based on a fictional story.

HÉCTOR TIZÓN was born in 1929 in the village of Yala, in the Andean Province of Jujuy, in the far northwest of Argentina. During high-school years in neighbouring Salta, he published his first stories in *El Intransigente,* a daily newspaper. After graduating in law from the University of La Plata in 1953, he returned to Jujuy and two years later was elected to the provincial legislature but never took his seat. In 1958 he entered the diplomatic service and became his country's cultural attaché in Mexico, where with others he founded the magazine *Síntesis* and published his first book. In 1960 he became consul in Milan but left diplomacy two years later and for a brief time was the Minister of Justice and Education in Jujuy, where he was also to practice law and edit a daily paper, *Proclama*. From 1976 to 1982, the years of the military coup, he lived in exile in Spain, where he worked for publishers, newspapers, and magazines. With several other writers he founded the literary magazine *Estaciones,* and he also edited a series of books on the Spanish Civil War based on accounts by foreign anti-Fascist authors. Since his return to Argentina he has divided his time between writing and his law office in San Salvador de Jujuy. His five novels, to date, are: *Fuego en Casabindo* (1969), *El cantar del profeta y el bandido* (1972), *Sota de bastos, caballo de espadas* (1975), *La casa y el viento* (1984), and *El hombre que llegó a un pueblo* (1988). He has also published three volumes of stories, *A un costado de los rieles* (1960), *El jactancioso y la bella* (1972), and *El traidor venerado* (1978). A fourth, *Recuento* (1984) is a selection from the earlier collections, together with three new stories. One of these is the tale included in this anthology.

Tizón has also published a volume of history, *La España borbónica* (1978). Two of his novels have appeared in French, and Gallimard is about to publish a third. Certain of his short fiction has appeared in German, Ukrainian, and Polish translations. He has twice appeared previously in English.

NOEMÍ ULLA is an author, scholar, and lecturer in contemporary River Plate literature at the University of Buenos Aires, from which she has a doctorate. She has also taught at the universities of Rosario and Morón and is currently engaged in scholarly work under the auspices of the Argentine research institute CONICET. Her fiction includes the two novels *Los que esperan el alba* (1967) and *Urdimbre* (1981), a collection of stories, *Ciudades* (1983), and the story *El ramito* (1990). Additionally, she has published book-length conversations with the writers Silvina Ocampo *(Encuentros con Silvina Ocampo* [1982]) and Adolfo Bioy-Casares *(Aventuras de la imaginación* [1990]) and, with Hugo Echave, a conversation with Graciela Fernández Meijide, one of the mothers of the Plaza de Mayo *(Después de la noche* [1986]). Ulla's other non-fictional books include a study of tango lyrics (*Tango, rebelión y nostalgia* [1967; revised, 1982]), critical examinations of writers (*Macedonio Fernández* [1980] and *Silvano Ocampo* [1981]), and a work on River Plate identity and colloquial language in the writers Borges, Arlt, Hernández, and Onetti *(Identidad rioplatense, 1930 – la escritura coloquial* [1990]). Born in Santa Fe, in 1933, Ulla studied literature at the University of Rosario and has lived in Buenos Aires since 1969. The story here, her second appearance in English, has not yet appeared in Spanish.

SUSAN ASHE, the co-translator, was born in India, in 1939, and came to live in England after Independence. Her version of Grazia Deledda's novel *After the Divorce* was published in London in 1985; with Norman Thomas di Giovanni she has also translated *Fellini's Casanova* (1977); an early volume of Borges essays, *Evaristo Carriego* (1984); a previous collection of Argentine short stories, *Celeste Goes Dancing* (1989); and the film script of Argentine director Luis Puenzo's adaptation of Albert Camus's *The Plague*.

NORMAN THOMAS DI GIOVANNI, born in Massachusetts in 1933, was invited to Buenos Aires in 1968 by Jorge Luis Borges, where the two worked together on translations of the Argentine writer's stories and poems into English. To date, this collaboration has resulted in eleven published volumes. Di Giovanni has translated many other Argentine writers. He edited a volume of the Anglo-Argentine Society's Jorge Luis Borges lectures – *In Memory of Borges* – for Constable in 1988 and the next year edited for them a collection of Argentine short stories, *Celeste Goes Dancing,* which he translated with Susan Ashe. Recently, in addition to working in Buenos Aires on the Chase Manhattan Bank's collection of contemporary Argentine painting, he edited and translated *Southern Memories,* a volume on the work of the Argentine artist Luis Fernando Benedit, and played a small part in Luis Puenzo's film adaptation of Camus's *Plague*. Di Giovanni also edited and introduced Andrew Graham-Yooll's *After the Despots* (1991). Since 1977, he has made his home in Devon.